Transfixed, she waited while that splintering gaze traveled upward, touching off explosions of honeyed fire deep in the hidden places of her body.

Sexuality, bold and predatory, smoldered in the clear pale depths of his eyes.

Heat stole through Ianthe, coloring her skin. Her eyes widened, became heavy lidded, drowsy with desire and invitation. Alex was watching her with half-lowered eyelids, sending delicious shivers through her.

"You look like a sea nymph," he said, the words rough and blunt. "I promised myself I wouldn't touch you, wouldn't let you get to me, but it was too late the first time I saw you."

ROBYN DONALD has always lived in Northland in New Zealand, initially on her father's stud dairy farm at Warkworth, then in the Bay of Islands, an area of great natural beauty, where she lives today with her husband and one corgi dog. She resigned her teaching position when she found she enjoyed writing romances more, and now spends any time not writing in reading, gardening, traveling and writing letters to keep up with her two adult children and her friends.

Books by Robyn Donald

Robyn Donald

FORBIDDEN PLEASURE

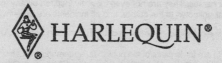

TORONTO • NEW YORK • LONDON
AMSTERDAM • PARIS • SYDNEY • HAMBURG
STOCKHOLM • ATHENS • TOKYO • MILAN • MADRID
PRAGUE • WARSAW • BUDAPEST • AUCKLAND

AUTHOR'S NOTE

The Kai Iwi lakes of Northland exist, and are more beautiful than I can describe, but I'm afraid you won't find this house beside one. There are no beaches, either, and although there is a motor camp, it doesn't have a shop. But it's a wonderful place to camp, and the water is an incredible color.

ISBN 0-373-12108-3

FORBIDDEN PLEASURE

First North American Publication 2000.

Copyright © 1998 by Robyn Donald.

Visit us at www.eHarlequin.com

Printed in U.S.A.

CHAPTER ONE

THE view, Ianthe Brown decided as she glowered through
the window, was picture pretty, everyone's idea of the tropics—dazzling white sand, water so blue it throbbed against
the hot air, gently waving trees. All that was missing was
the sound of surf on the reef and the traditional happy-
go-lucky attitude of the Polynesians who lived on those
smiling, palm-tasselled islands. And the palms.

Not surprising, since they were two thousand kilometres
to the north of this northern part of New Zealand.

Ianthe frowned at the fingermarks on her reddened wrist,
then stooped to massage her aching leg. The man who'd
jerked her out of that haven of tranquillity and escorted her
into this house was as far removed from happy-go-lucky as
anyone could be; his mission had been to get her inside so
someone else could interview her, whether she wanted that
or not. Normally she'd have torn verbal strips off him; a
sleepless night and the drugged pleasure of having at last
closed her eyes and drifted into unconsciousness had tem-
porarily scrambled her brain.

It was back in full working order now, and she was furious.

Of course she could climb through the window and run
away, but she had no taste for humiliation; in her present
state she'd be ludicrously easy to catch.

She surveyed the room with critical eyes. Luxuriously
spare, it oozed the kind of casual perfection that proclaimed
both megabucks and a very good interior decorator. What
little she'd noticed of the rest of the house revealed the
same sophisticated simplicity.

A far cry, she thought ironically, from her spartan quarters of the past few years. The cabin on the schooner had been so small she'd been able to stand in the middle and touch all four sides without too much stretching.

Absently she transferred her weight to her good leg. Five minutes ago she'd been sound asleep in the shade of the pines, only to be hauled off her rug by an idiot with a manner cribbed from the more mindless and violent films, who'd ignored her vigorous objections and frogmarched her the hundred metres to a house she hadn't noticed.

Had she, Ianthe wondered with a shiver of foreboding as she straightened, stumbled into one of those films?

No, this was New Zealand. Mafia godfathers didn't exist here.

Awareness prickled across the back of her neck. Without moving—without breathing—she strained to see from the corner of her eyes. On the very edge of her vision waited the tall, lean shadow of a man, intimidating and silent. A mindless panic tightening her skin, she set her teeth and turned.

She'd expected the frogmarcher, but the man who watched her with narrowed, icy eyes—eyes so pale in his tanned face that her stomach jumped—was an infinitely more threatening proposition. Such eyes, Ianthe thought on a swift, involuntary breath, could indicate an Anglo-Saxon heritage, except that the strong, dark features were cast in a far more exotic mould—Italian, perhaps.

'Who,' she asked steadily, 'are you, and what right do you have to kidnap me?'

Although something flickered in the brilliant gaze, his expression didn't alter. Urbanely he asked, 'Don't you have laws against trespassing in New Zealand?'

He spoke like an Oxford-educated Englishman, each clipped, curt word at subtle variance with the deep, rich voice, textured by the maverick hint of an accent she couldn't place.

About six feet tall, he was startlingly good-looking, the angular, autocratic face emphasised by a forceful jaw and a hard, deceptively beautiful mouth. Yet the ice-blue eyes—piercing as lasers, wholly without warmth—dominated his tanned features, and beneath that uncompromising exterior Ianthe sensed vitality, a fierce energy barely contained by his will-power.

Into her mind sprang the sudden glittering image of a hawk high in a summer sky, poised against the shimmering incandescence for a moment out of time before it plummeted lethally to earth and its prey.

Beautifully cut shirt and trousers fitted him with the casual elegance of excellent tailoring. Irritated, Ianthe realised that if he'd been clad in scruffy jeans and a shirt off the peg he'd be just as imperious and formidable and dangerously compelling.

In old shorts and a loose T-shirt that had faded into shabbiness, she must look downmarket and conspicuous. Her chin lifted a fraction of an inch. 'Trespassing laws in New Zealand are lenient. Anyway, these lakes are reserves.'

'Not this one. The land around it is privately owned—as you are well aware. You had to climb over a locked gate to get here.'

Ianthe had wondered, but her need for solitude had been greater than her curiosity. She drew in a deep breath. For the first time since she'd woken in hospital with over a hundred stitches in her leg she felt alive, every cell in her body alert and flooded with adrenalin.

'Whatever,' she countered, 'it still doesn't give your henchman the right to manhandle me. All he's entitled to do is tell me to get off your property. If I'd refused to go after that you might have a case, although it's probably only fair to warn you that you'd have to prove I'd done some damage before any court would take you seriously.'

'It sounds as though you make a habit of trespassing.'

Ianthe stared at him.

'You know so much about your rights,' he elaborated, a lurking note of sarcasm biting into her composure.

Crisply she retorted, 'I once worked for a summer with

the Department of Conservation, where you soon learn all about the laws of trespassing. By dragging me here, your offsider has put himself well and truly in the wrong. The New Zealand police don't take a kindly view of assault. As he knows, because he's a New Zealander himself.'

She didn't hold up her reddened wrist, or even look at it, but the man's gaze fastened onto her skin and something explosive splintered its cold clarity before the long lashes, dark as jealousy, covered his eyes again. 'Did he hurt you?' he asked in a voice that pulled every tiny hair upright over her body.

'No.'

He came across the room with silent speed. Ianthe watched with bewilderment as he picked up her hand and looked at her wrist. A chill tightened her skin, jerked with sickening impact in the depths of her stomach.

'He's bruised you,' he said slowly.

Feeling strangely sorry for the frogmarcher, Ianthe said, 'I bruise very easily, and he didn't hurt me. In fact, he did this when I stumbled. He stopped me from falling into the water.'

Her voice faded. Looking down at the contrast of dark fingers locked around the delicate whiteness of her wrist, she swallowed and pulled away; he resisted a moment, then the long fingers loosened and she was free. Completely unnerved by his reaction, she took a stumbling step backwards and leaned heavily against the windowsill.

'I'm sorry,' he said with a frigid remoteness.

Quickly, her voice oddly gruff, she said with stubborn insistence, 'Besides, I was on the Queen's Chain.'

'The Queen's Chain?' he asked silkily, pinning her with that laser glance.

Sensation slithered the length of Ianthe's spine. Doing her best to ignore it, she replied didactically, 'In New Zealand almost all waterways are surrounded by the Queen's Chain. The land twenty metres back from the water's edge, although used by the landowner, is actually owned by the Crown—specifically so that people have access.'

'Your Queen is a landowner indeed,' he said softly, not attempting to hide the mockery in his words. 'And to get to that Queen's Chain you had to cross private property.'

Your Queen, so he wasn't English. Her confident tone belying her hollow stomach, Ianthe snapped, 'Possibly, but I wasn't trespassing when that idiot decided to prove what a big, tough man he is by dragging me here.'

Ianthe was of medium height, but a year in and out of hospital had stripped flesh from her bones so that she weighed less than she had for the last five years. She'd been no match at all for a frogmarcher built like a rugby forward.

His boss smiled at her. 'He'll apologise,' he said.

How could a mere movement of muscles transform aloof arrogance into something so charismatic? He looked like a Renaissance princeling, at once blazingly attractive yet dangerous, cultured yet barbaric, his handsome features strengthened by the disciplined ruthlessness underpinning them.

'You are,' he went on, 'quite right, and I apologise for Mark's rather officious protection of my privacy. He had no right to touch you or haul you in here.'

Ianthe suspected that behind that spell-binding face was a keen brain that had rapidly chosen this response, knowing it would soothe her. In other words, she thought sturdily, she was being manipulated.

After returning his smile with one of her own—detached, she hoped, and coolly dismissive—she said, 'New Zealanders love their country, and one reason is because they can go almost wherever they like in it.'

'Subject, one assumes, to the laws of the countryside? Closing gates and so forth?'

'Of course,' she said, knowing that she'd left no gate undone behind her.

Dark lashes drooped, narrowing the pale gaze. 'To make up a little for Mark's unceremonious intrusion into your life, can I offer you a drink? Tea, perhaps, or something alcoholic if you'd prefer that? And then I'll take you back to your car.'

Stiffly, nerves still jangling from the after-effects of that smile, Ianthe said, 'No, thank you. I'm not thirsty.'

'I can understand that you have no wish to stay in a house where you underwent such an unpleasant experience,' he said smoothly, 'but I'd like to show you that I'm not some Mafia don on holiday.'

Her glance flashed to his unreadable face. Could he read her mind? No, of course not. She'd barely articulated the thought.

Off balance, she said hastily, 'I'm sure you're not—'

'Then let me make whatever amends I can.'

Charm was a rare gift, and an unfair one. When backed by pure steel it was almost unforgivable. Reluctant, angry because her leg was threatening imminent collapse, Ianthe said, 'You don't need to make amends, but—I'd like a cup of tea, thank you.'

'It would be my pleasure.'

She eased herself away from the window and limped towards him, waiting for signs of shock. But the ice-blue gaze remained fixed on her face, although he took her elbow in an impersonal grip.

He'd probably blench when he saw the scar, she thought savagely, but she was used to that.

The long tanned fingers at her elbow lent confidence as well as support. They also sent a slow pulse of excitement through her. Of course she didn't allow herself to lean on him as he escorted her through the door, across a hall floored with pale Italian ceramic tiles and into a breathtaking room where the light from the lake played across superb angles and planes and surfaces.

'Oh!' Ianthe said, abruptly stopping.

His fingers tightened a moment on her elbow, then relaxed. 'What is it?'

'Nothing.' Feeling foolish, she explained lamely, 'The lake looks wonderful from here.'

He urged her across to a comfortable seat. 'It looks wonderful from any vantage point,' he said. 'I've travelled widely, but I don't think I've ever seen anything like the colour of this water.'

Ianthe sat down, keeping her face averted. Glass doors had been pushed right back to reveal a wide terrace and the brilliant beach. 'It's because it's a dune lake,' she said. 'The white sand reflects the sky more intensely.'

'Whatever causes it, it's beautiful,' he said, sitting down in a chair close by. 'But then, New Zealand is a glorious country. So varied a landscape, usually with mountains to back up each magnificent vista.'

'Mountains are all very well in the background, but that's where they should stay. Give me a nice warm beach any day.' A year ago she'd have meant it.

His considering glance fomented a disturbing, forbidden pleasure deep within her. They were so distant, those eyes, so dispassionately at variance with his warm Mediterranean colouring. Bronze skin and blue-black hair sharpened the impact of their frosty intensity, until she felt their impact like an earthquake, inescapable, terrifying.

In an amused voice he said, 'You don't look as though anything much frightens you.'

'I like to be warm,' she said, thinking, If you only knew! 'I was born in Northland, so I'm not used to snow.'

'Yet water can be cold.'

He still hadn't looked at her leg, but Ianthe wished fervently that she'd chosen to wear trousers rather than shorts. She had no illusions about the ugliness of the puckered, distorted skin that ran almost the full length of her leg. Although future plastic surgery would tidy it up, it would always be there, a jagged, unlovely reminder of past pain.

'Only if you're silly enough to keep swimming after you start to shiver,' she said, adding drily, 'And unless you're swimming in the Arctic, it's nowhere near as cold as snow.

Of course, where you come from the mountains all have either a rack railway up the side or a hotel perched on top. Or both. It makes them hard to take seriously.'

Strong white teeth flashed for a second as he smiled. 'So you didn't enjoy the European Alps,' he said blandly. 'Although I was born in Europe, I spent much of my youth in Australia.' His eyes glimmered. 'No mountains there, nothing much but sky.'

'I've never been to either place, but I've seen photos.'

'Perhaps it's a human characteristic to want to tame those things that threaten us.' His gaze moved slowly over her face, rested a tingling fraction of a second on her soft mouth, then flicked to the tumbled bounty of her hair, its gentle, honey-coloured waves streaked with natural highlights the colour of untarnished copper. In a cool, speculative voice he continued, 'I don't think mountains in New Zealand have either railways or restaurants, do they?'

Her nerves jumping, she said huskily, 'Not to the summit, no.'

The door opened. Ianthe watched warily as Mark the frogmarcher, fair and with the solid, blocky body of a surfer, carried in a tea-tray. Her host—whoever he was—must have given the order before he'd seen her, Ianthe thought, wondering why she let herself be irritated at such blatant damage control.

Mark set the tray down on the table close to her chair, then moved the table so that she didn't have to reach. Both tea and coffee, she noticed. He'd left nothing to chance.

'I hope you will pour,' the owner said.

'Yes, of course.'

Standing back, Mark said woodenly, 'I'm sorry if I frightened you, but you were trespassing.'

With equal formality, Ianthe said, 'Property rights don't confer manhandling privileges, but I accept your apology.'

Summoning her most limpid smile, she directed it at him until colour rose in his skin. He sent a swift, frowning glance to his employer, who said, 'Thank you, Mark.' With an abrupt nod the younger man turned jerkily and left the room.

Her host laughed quietly. 'You New Zealanders!' he murmured. 'I'd say the honours went to you that time.'

With an unwilling smile Ianthe poured tea with a strong, tarry smell. When she asked what sort it was, he answered, 'Lapsang souchong—Chinese tea. Don't you like it? Shall I get another—?'

'No, no,' she interrupted. 'I just haven't come across it before. I like trying new things.'

He waited while she sipped it, and smiled lazily when she said, 'It's different, but I like it.'

'Good,' he said, and picked up the cup he'd collected from her. 'Are you a local, or holidaying like me?'

'I'm on holiday.'

'At the camping ground?'

'No, I'm staying in a bach.' His lifted brows led her to enlarge, 'In New Zealand a bach is a small, rather scruffy beach house.'

His scrutiny shredded the fragile barrier of her confidence. Ianthe stopped herself from blinking defensively; whenever he looked at her something very strange happened in the pit of her stomach, a kind of drawing sensation that hardened into an ache.

Dourly she told herself that he probably had an equally powerful effect on any woman under a hundred. Those eyes were hypnotic. Perhaps he was conducting a subtle interrogation; if so, he'd mistaken his adversary. He hadn't told her who he was, so she wouldn't tell him anything about herself.

Childish, but she felt threatened, and defiance was as good a reaction as any.

He broke into her thoughts by saying, 'Ah, those small houses near the camping ground.'

'Yes.'

'I heard that they're under threat.'

Ianthe nodded. 'They're built on what's now reserve

land. The owners aren't allowed to alter the buildings beyond any necessary repairs, and when they die the baches
will be torn down and the land returned to the Crown.'

'And is yours a family bach?'

She said warily, 'It's owned by friends.'

He changed the subject with smooth confidence. 'I hope
the weather stays as idyllic as it's been for the past couple
of weeks.'

'It should, but Northland—all of New Zealand, in
fact—is a forecaster's nightmare. The country's long and
narrow, and because it's where the tropics meet the cold
air coming up from the Antarctic we get weather from
every direction. Still, it's high summer, so with any luck
we'll have glorious weather until the end of February.' The
pedantic note in her voice was her only defence against his
speculative, probing gaze.

She added, 'Unless another cyclone comes visiting from
the north, of course. We've already had two this holiday
season, although neither of them amounted to more than
heavy rain.'

'Let's hope the tropics keep their cyclones to themselves,' he said, giving no indication of how long he intended to stay.

After that they spoke more generalities—conversation
that meant nothing, revealed nothing, was not intended to
be taken seriously or recalled. Yet beneath the surface ca-
sualness and ease there were deeper, questionable currents,
and whenever she looked up he was watching her.

Eventually Ianthe put down her empty cup and said,
'That was lovely, thank you. I'd better be getting back.'

'Certainly.' He got to his feet with loose-limbed masculine grace. 'I'll drive you to your car.'

'I can walk,' she said automatically.

Without taking his eyes from her face he asked, 'And
make your leg even more painful?'

She grimaced, because it had now begun to throb, and
she knew that the only way to keep it from getting worse

was to lie down. 'All right,' she said reluctantly, adding, 'Thank you very much.'

'It's very little recompense for Mark's officiousness.'

He'd come to take her elbow again. Ianthe knew that his fingers didn't burn her skin as he helped her up, but that was what it felt like. 'Mark's responsible for that,' she said tersely, tightening her lips against the odd, shivery sensations running through her.

'He's employed by me,' he said, 'so I'm responsible.'

Ianthe took a few stiff steps, her limp becoming more pronounced as the ache in her leg suddenly intensified.

He said something under his breath, and with an economy of movement that shocked her, lifted her in his arms.

'Hey!' she exclaimed, unable to say anything more as a secret, feverish excitement swallowed her up.

'Perhaps you'd rather Mark carried you,' he said, locking her against his hard-muscled torso with casual strength as he strode with surprising ease towards the wide hall that led to a big front door.

The promise of masculine power hadn't been an illusion. The self-control that gave authority to his spectacular, hawkish good looks had been transmuted into sheer, determined energy.

An alarming combination of flame and ice electrified Ianthe. Striving to sound level and prosaic, she said, 'I don't need to be carried.'

'You're as white as a sheet and sweat is standing out on your forehead. Please don't try to make me feel worse than I already do.'

Because Ianthe hated being pitied she returned coldly, 'I'm not. My leg hurts, but I'd get there.'

'Even if you had to crawl,' he said with caustic disapproval. 'Cutting off your nose to spite your face not only wastes time, it turns perfectly legitimate sympathy into intense irritation.'

Which left her with nothing to say. Clearly he did feel

responsible for his henchman's behaviour, but Mark's macho hijacking no longer concerned her.

Her heart jumped as she stole a glance at the splendid profile, outlined by an unexpected blaze of gold as they stepped out of the door beneath a skylight. Attraction, she told herself with contemptuous bravado. It's just attraction—that common meeting point between male and female. It means nothing.

Bracing herself against it, she forced her attention away from him and onto her surroundings.

Whoever had designed the house had understood Northland's climate. A *porte-cochère* extended from the door across the gravel drive, offering shelter from summer's heat as well as from the downpours that could batter the peninsula at any season. In its shade waited a Range Rover, large and luxurious and dusty.

'I'll have to put you down,' her host said, and did so with exquisite care.

She clutched at the handle of the vehicle, and for a second his arms tightened around her again. Her bones heated, slackened, melted in the swift warmth of his embrace and the faint, potently masculine tang she'd been carefully not registering. He waited until she let go of the door handle and straightened up, then stepped back.

'Can you manage?' he enquired evenly as he opened the door.

'Yes.' Refusing to acknowledge the ache in her leg, she climbed in, took a deep, steadying breath and reached down to clip on her seatbelt. She didn't look at the man who walked around to his side and got in.

'I presume you left your car at the gate,' he said as he started the engine.

'Yes. In the pull-off.'

He handled the big machine with skill on the narrow gravel road. Ianthe sat silently until she saw her car huddled against a pine plantation, shielded from the dusty road by a thick growth of teatree and scrub.

'Here,' she said.

'I see it.' He drove in behind her car and stopped.

As she got quickly down and limped across to her elderly Japanese import, Ianthe repressed an ironic smile. The only things her car shared with the opulent Rover were the basic equipment and a coat of dust.

The sun had sailed far enough across the sky to bypass the dark shade of the trees and heat up the car's interior. With a last uncharitable thought for Mark, Ianthe wound down windows and held the door open, wishing desperately that her unwilling host would just get back into his big vehicle and leave her alone. She felt balanced on a knife-edge, her past hidden by shadow, her future almost echoing with emptiness.

'There, that's cool enough,' she said with a bright smile. 'Thank you.'

'I should be thanking you for not prosecuting me,' he said, amusement glimmering for a second in the frigid depths of his eyes. 'The only recompense I can make is to offer the beach to you whenever you wish to swim.'

'That's very kind of you—thank you.' The words were clumsy and she couldn't keep the surprise from her voice, so she nodded and retreated to her car, thinking, Not likely.

Pity had produced that offer, and she loathed pity. Since the accident she'd endured more than a lifetime's quota, defended from its enfeebling effects only by a stubborn, mute pride.

With a savage twist she switched on the engine, furious when it grumbled and stuttered before coughing into silence. Thin-lipped, she tried it again, and this time it caught and purred into life. Smiling politely, she waved.

Before she let the brake off he leaned forward. 'I'll follow you home, just to make sure you're all right.'

'There's no need,' she began, but he'd already stepped back and headed towards the Rover.

Unease crept across her skin on sinister cat's paws. For a moment she even toyed with the idea of going to someone else's bach, until common sense scoffed that a few questions would soon tell him where she lived.

She wasn't scared—she had no reason to fear him.

So she drove sedately down the road until she came to the third bach by the second lake, and turned through the shade of the huge macrocarpa cypress on the front lawn, then into the garage. The Range Rover drew to a halt on the road outside, its engine purring while she got out of the car, locked it, and went towards the door of the bach.

He waited until she'd actually unlocked it before tooting once and turning around.

The last Ianthe saw of him was an arrogant, angular profile against the swirling white dust from the road and the negligent wave of one long hand. Her breath hissed out. For a moment she stared at the faded paint on the door, then jerkily opened it and went inside.

Heat hit her like a blow. Pushing wide the windows, she thought briefly of the wall of glass, open to the lake and the air, then shrugged. When this bach had been built bifold windows that turned rooms into pavilions had not been a part of the ordinary house, let alone a holiday place like this.

Who was he? And why did he feel the need for someone like Mark in a place like New Zealand? Perhaps, she thought, curling her lip, he had a fragile ego that demanded the reassurance of a bodyguard.

It didn't seem likely, but then what did she know of the very rich? Or the very beautiful? If the camera liked his face as much as her eyes had, he might well be a film star. As it was, his face had seemed vaguely familiar, like a half-remembered image from a stranger's photograph album.

From now on she was going to have to confine herself to the shore of this lake, which meant curious looks and often audible comments about her leg. She looked down at the scar. Purple-red, jagged and uneven, it stretched from her thigh to her ankle. She'd damned near died from shock and loss of blood. Sometimes she even wished she had.

Her capacity for self-pity sickened her. It was new to her, this enormous waste of sullen desperation that so often lay in wait like quicksand.

Determinedly cheerful, she said out loud into the stifling air, 'Well, Ianthe Brown, you've had an experience. Whoever he is, he's not your common or garden tourist.'

Lifting heavy waves of hair from her hot scalp, she headed for the bathroom.

Tricia Upham, the friend whose parents owned the bach and had lent it to Ianthe for as long as she needed it, had said as she handed over the key, 'Now that your hair's grown past your shoulders, for heaven's sake leave it alone. Chopping it off and hiding it behind goggles and flippers was just wicked ingratitude.'

'Long hair's a nuisance when you spend a lot of time underwater in a wetsuit,' Ianthe had replied.

Now it didn't seem as though she'd ever get back into a wetsuit.

In fact, she'd be glad if she could just get into the water. Setting her jaw, she washed her face and towelled it dry. 'Self-pity is a refuge for wimps,' she told her reflection, challenging the weakness inside her.

Soon she'd be able to swim again.

Surely.

She only needed determination.

The man behind the desk called out, 'Come in.'

Mark appeared. 'Before you tell me how big a fool I am,' he said stiffly, 'I'm sorry.'

The frown that had been gathering behind Alex Considine's eyes vanished. He smiled with irony. 'Just don't let your enthusiasm override your common sense again.'

'I won't.'

'If you see anything suspicious, report to me.' His smile broadened. 'I gather my mother got to you.'

Mark grinned and relaxed. 'Several times,' he said, adding, 'She said you were in danger and emphasised that I should treat everyone with suspicion.'

So why bring a trespasser into the house? Alex wondered drily. Still, his mother was very persuasive, and Mark was a caretaker, not a bodyguard. 'She's spent her life worrying about me. I'm not in danger, especially not from slight young women of about twenty-five with a limp. Don't take any notice of my mother.'

He hadn't been able to convince her that, although there were people who'd rejoice at the news of his death, nothing was likely to happen to him in New Zealand. It had its problems, this little South Pacific country, and was fighting the worldwide increase in crime like every other country, but a man was probably as safe here as he would be any-where.

He looked down at the pile of faxes on his desk and asked, 'Who is the trespasser?'

Mark gave him a startled look. 'How did you know I recognised her?'

'If she'd been the usual tourist you'd have escorted her to the gate and sent her on her way.'

'Yeah, well, I knew I'd seen her somewhere, and I knew it was on television, so I thought she was a reporter. That's why I brought her back here. I thought you might want to interrogate her.'

Alex Considine nodded. 'But?'

'When I came in with the tea-tray I remembered who she was. She fronted a series of wildlife documentaries a year or so ago, until she got bitten by a shark somewhere up in the Pacific.'

So that was what had given her the limp and that hideous scar. Alex's blood chilled. 'What's her name?'

'Ianthe Brown. For a while she turned up on all the covers of the women's magazines. She lost her job after she got bitten, of course.' He shrugged. 'The girl they got to replace her looks just as good in a bikini, but she's not as good in her job. You could tell Ianthe Brown really liked what she was doing.'

Alex nodded, and Mark said, 'By the way, I didn't mean to hurt her wrist. She almost fell into the water and then she just lost it—started to shake and went as white as a sheet. Scared the hell out of me, so I hauled her out a bit too roughly. But I didn't mean to hurt her,' he repeated bluntly.

'She's probably nervous in the water,' Alex said. 'After an attack like that, anyone would be.'

'Well, yeah, she might be, although we don't have any sharks in the lakes.'

Alex laughed. 'It's not quite so easy as that,' he said drily. 'All right, on your way.'

'What time do you want dinner?'

'Eight.' He was already looking at the first paper, and barely heard the door close behind the other man.

An hour later he lifted his head and got up, walking out onto the deck. The lake danced before him, ripely blue as the sheen on a kingfisher's wings, and he summoned the face of the woman.

Intriguing, he thought.

But he'd known women who were more than intriguing, who exuded sexual promise with every smile, every movement of their bodies. This one wasn't like that. Oh, she had a good figure and skin, and her golden eyes were miraculous, but she limped badly, and although she had regular, neat features she wasn't beautiful in the modern sense.

He frowned. At first those hot amber eyes had glittered with anger, the long dark lashes almost hiding the wariness. And that hair! Hair to tangle around a man's heart, he thought sardonically, knowing his was safe. This was a more primitive reaction; he wanted to see her hair spread out on his pillow, that delicately sensuous mouth blurred by his kisses, those eyes heavy and slumbrous with passion.

When their eyes had met, his stomach had contracted as though he'd been punched in the solar plexus. A savage, unmanageable physical desire had bypassed defences set up and reinforced since early adolescence.

Using the cold, analytical brain that served him so well, he recalled her face, her defiant stance, the square chin, the gentle, womanly curves—and watched his hands clench in front of him as his body responded helplessly.

What quality in her summoned such a response? She'd had no tricks, no artifice. The soft mouth had been naked of lipstick, and the glinting eyes hadn't been emphasised by mascara and eyeshadow. Yet beneath her delicate, slightly old-fashioned prettiness he'd sensed a smouldering intensity, a primitive carnal power that threatened while it beckoned.

What had those amazing eyes seen when she'd looked at him the first time?

Grimacing, he forced his hands to relax. She'd seen what he saw in the mirror every morning—the face that proclaimed his pedigree and announced his heritage, features that could be traced back a thousand years.

Those great eyes had viewed him with nothing but suspicion, he thought, trying to find something amusing in that, a thread of irony that would quench the fever curling through his loins.

Her cool composure had challenged the primitive, fundamental male in him, as had her burning, golden eyes and her pale skin and that hair. And, he thought ironically, the body beneath those appalling clothes. Oh, yes, he'd responded fiercely to the slim legs and the sleek, lithe curves of breast and hip, the oddly fragile line of her throat and the thin wrists and ankles.

Different, but just as fierce, had been his reaction to that abomination of a scar, to her limp, to the pain in her eyes and the pallor of her face when her leg hurt. That unwilling, highly suspect need to protect her shocked him.

He was a man of strong passions and even stronger control. Celibacy was no stranger to him. And he was, he admitted, cynical about women, and regrettably bored with professional beauties.

Yet when he'd opened the door and seen her staring out of the window, her long legs and neat little backside revealed by her shorts, somewhere at a deep, cellular level he'd responded with a white-hot leap of recognition.

Damned inconvenient, he thought caustically, walking back into the room to straighten the pile of papers beside the laptop computer. He might crave the physical release of sex, but now, of all times, he needed to keep his mind clear.

For a moment he summoned the face and gorgeously voluptuous body of a woman who would have been furious to hear herself described as a call girl, but who would, he knew, be on the next flight if he asked her. His mouth tightened. He had no illusions; apart from his power and his money, Isabel wanted him because he had never succumbed to her lush expertise. He'd never used women, and his irritating desire for the interesting intruder wasn't going to drive him in that direction.

There were other, far more important things to think about. That was why he'd come to New Zealand—to think. The decision he had to make would affect not only his life, but those of millions.

And for the only time since he'd grown up he couldn't weigh the facts and measure the results of any given decision. His self-contained mind—razor-sharp and cold-blooded he'd been called often enough to make the terms clichés—didn't even want to face the prospect.

The finely etched features of Ianthe Brown coalesced in the recesses of his brain. The contrast between her elaborate first name and her prosaic surname amused him. Ianthe meant violet flower, although the first Ianthe, his classical education reminded him, had been a Greek nymph, the daughter of Oceanus and Tethys.

All suspiciously appropriate.

Those delicately etched features were the sort adored by

the camera. He caught himself wondering if the camera also revealed that latent wildness in her. Had she ever indulged it? Or was she a passionate puritan, afraid to give rein to her emotions?

Frowning, he looked out of the window and across the impossibly blue water of the lake. Once Mark had told him who she was it had been easy to find out more about her. The investigator in Auckland had worked fast and the pages had come through on the fax a few minutes ago.

Nothing, however, about her personal life. Apparently when featured by the women's magazines she'd spoken only about her work, which had seemed to consist of swimming decoratively with whales and dolphins.

And sharks. No doubt the tense line of her succulent mouth and the frequent opacity of her eyes were other, more subtle results of that attack.

Once again gripped by a ferocious instinct to protect her, he pressed the buzzer beside the desk, then put the detective's findings into a drawer.

When Mark appeared he said, 'You're going into Dargaville tomorrow morning, aren't you? Go to the video shop and get me any that have Ianthe Brown in them.'

When he was alone again he picked up the papers on his desk and began to read, banishing memories of a passionately sculpted mouth, and hair the mixed colours of gold and new-minted copper, and skin translucent and delicate as silk.

And huge golden eyes that reflected the sheen of firelight and hinted at passions he'd never waken.

CHAPTER TWO

AFTER a restless, dream-hounded night, Ianthe drank two cups of tea and forced herself to eat a slice of toast before driving down to the nearest town, the sleepy little port of Dargaville on the wide reaches of the Northern Wairoa River.

When she'd stocked up on the groceries that weren't available in the small shop at the motor camp, she bought a couple of magazines and tried hard to resist several new paperbacks. Succumbing, she appeased her conscience by buying another four from the reject rack at the library.

About halfway home she saw a Range Rover pushed sideways into the ditch. A familiar figure stood beside it, surveying the damage.

She almost put her foot down and accelerated past Mark the frogmarcher, but in some odd way his behaviour had formed a tenuous bond between them, so she drew in behind and got out. 'Hello,' she said coolly. 'Are you all right?'

Mark stood unsmiling. 'I'm fine.'

Wondering why she'd bothered, Ianthe persevered, 'Do you want me to call in at the Kaihu garage for you?'

'Everything's under control,' he told her, 'but you could do me a favour—I've got frozen goods, and although they're well-wrapped they aren't going to last. Would you drop them off at the house?'

He must have decided she was relatively harmless. Fighting down an odd sense of darkening destiny, Ianthe said crisply, 'Yes, I'll do that. Will you need a ride back after the Rover's been towed to the garage?'

'No.'

'All right,' she said, still feeling that she was burning unknown bridges behind her. 'Hand over the frozen stuff and I'll deliver it.'

Five minutes later she was on her way, with a large plastic bag in the boot of her car and a frown pulling at the smooth skin above her brows. If she'd had any common sense at all she'd have driven on past, but she was too imbued with the New Zealand instinct to help.

And now she had to beard the lion in his den—no, the hawk in his nest.

Perhaps hawks had eyries, like eagles, she thought with a faint smile, flicking down the visor as the sun shimmered like a mirage on the tarseal in front of her. A hawk in a summer sky, proud and fierce and lethal...

And handsome. That disturbing familiarity tugging at her mind was probably instinctive female homage to an ideal of masculine beauty. The arrangement of his features pleased some integral pattern set up by the human brain so she recognised him as good-looking.

Logical, when you thought it through.

A too-fast swerve around the next corner banished the enigma of her unwilling host of the previous day. From then on she concentrated, driving past the other three lakes and the locked gate that separated the reserve from the fourth lake in its nest of pines, along a road with farms on one side and the sombre green of the plantation on the other, until she made a right-angle turn over a cattlestop onto a very ordinary drive. It didn't look as though a man of mystery lived at the end of it.

As she drew up under that splendid *porte-cochère* every cell in Ianthe's body thrummed with a hidden excitement, heating her skin and sharpening her senses.

She got out and rang the doorbell to the accompaniment of the busy, high-pitched chattering of a fantail fluttering amongst the gold-spotted aurelia leaves. Instead of the rich golden brown of the common variety, this one was sooty, with a breast of dark chocolate, the comical white brow and collar missing. Ianthe wasn't a bird person, but she knew enough about the small, cheerful birds to be aware that black fantails were unusual in the North Island.

Its complete lack of fear and its sombre colouring shouldn't have lifted the hair on the back of her neck. Although she was aware of the bird's Maori reputation as a harbinger of death, she was a scientist, for heaven's sake. Yet, as she stood before the big wooden door, the fantail seemed like a magic messenger, the emissary from another world who summons the hero to a quest.

How's that for logical, professional thinking? she mocked. Darwin would be proud of you.

With a shrug she turned to ring the bell again, but before her finger touched it the door opened silently and the man who had haunted her sleep looked at her.

Something flared in the light eyes, a response she couldn't read; it was instantly replaced by an aloof withdrawal.

Stung, she summoned a glib professional smile. 'I have some frozen groceries that your—chauffeur asked me to deliver.'

The frown remained, albeit reduced to a pleat of the black brows. His eyes revealed nothing but shimmering silver depths, cold and lucent. 'Thank you.'

He walked beside her to the car. 'Which are the frozen goods? I'll get them.' Straightening with the plastic bag, he told her, 'Mark got pushed into the ditch by a truck that was avoiding a dog. Thank you for being a good samaritan.'

So he'd known she was on her way. She said lightly, 'You can't compare delivering a parcel of frozen peas to rescuing a man who fell among thieves. I'd better be off. I hope all goes well with the Rover.'

Ianthe couldn't read any emotion in his expression or his tone. Silence stretched between them, taut, obscurely equivocal.

Evenly, without emphasis, he said, 'Come and have something to drink. You look hot and tired and thirsty.'

A flicker of movement from the little fantail caught Ianthe's eye. Perched on the topmost twig of the leafy plant, the bird spread its tail feathers, black plumage a startling contrast to green and gold leaves. Round, bright eyes seemed to fix onto Ianthe, insistent, commanding.

It was stupid to give any significance to such a tiny creature, seen almost every day in New Zealand. It would be even more stupid to accept this invitation.

Yet some impulse, a heartbeat away from refusal, changed her mind. Slowly she said, 'That sounds wonderful. I am hot and tired and thirsty.'

He smiled, and her heart flipped. 'But perhaps we should be introduced first,' he said, and held out his free hand. 'I'm Alex Considine.'

She knew that name! She just couldn't place it. On a subtly exhaled breath she said, 'I'm Ianthe Brown,' and with a kind of resignation put her hand into his.

The moment it closed over hers a wildfire response stormed through her, drowning out common sense and caution. Dizzily she thought that the handshake was a claiming, a symbolic gesture of possession taken and granted.

Ridiculous, she thought, panicking. Utterly ridiculous!

Possibly she jerked her hand away, but he let it go as though women who shivered when he touched them weren't uncommon in his life.

It probably happened all the time, she thought, and said inanely, 'How do you do?'

'How do you do, Miss Brown?' he said, amusement deepening his voice. 'Come in. Is there anything you want to bring with you? Some frozen goods, perhaps, to add to mine in the freezer?'

Damn! She should have dropped her meat off on the way here. But, no, she'd been so excited at the prospect of seeing him again she'd driven mindlessly past the turn-off.

'Actually, yes, there is,' she admitted, grateful to be able to stoop and lift her parcel from the car.

Adding it to his, he motioned her to go ahead. Chin tilted, she obeyed, saying with a casual smile, 'Miss Brown sounds incredibly formal. I answer better to Ianthe.'

His lashes drooped for a micro-second. 'Then you must call me Alex,' he said, and showed her into the sitting room with its wonderful view of the beach and the lake. 'If you don't mind waiting, I'll put these in the freezer.'

He was not, Ianthe thought as she walked across to the open doors and squinted at the violent contrast of white sand against the bold blue of the water, the sort of man you offered to help.

Cicadas played their tiny penetrating zithers in the branches of the trees behind the house. The familiar noise set Ianthe's nerves jumping; trying to centre herself, she took a few deep breaths, but her skin tightened. She turned a little clumsily, and there was Alex coming in through the door with a tray that held bottles of various sorts.

'I can make tea or coffee if you'd prefer either,' he said when she glanced at the tray.

Ianthe shook her head. 'No, something cold would be wonderful,' she said gratefully.

'Come outside; it's marginally cooler.'

A terrace stretched along the front of the house, and there, shaded by the roof, was a sitting-out area—comfortable white squabs and cushions on long benches. Above, a pergola draped with vines shaded eyes from the vibrating intensity of the sun. It was completely private. You could, Ianthe thought enviously, lie naked on those squabs and let the sun soak bone deep.

Unfortunately she couldn't risk it with skin as pale as hers. Not so Alex Considine, whose darker skin would only deepen in colour under the sun's caress. However, his aura of leashed energy made it difficult to imagine him lying around with no aim but to polish up his tan.

Her stomach contracting at the images that flashed across

her far too co-operative brain, she asked swiftly, 'Why did you decide to come here for your holidays, Alex?'

He answered readily enough. 'I wanted somewhere peaceful where I wouldn't run into anyone I knew. What would you like—orange juice, lime, or something else?'

His explanation was, Ianthe thought shrewdly, the truth, but not the whole truth. 'Lime, thank you.'

Accepting the glass he handed her, she observed, 'I bet before you go home you'll have tripped over someone you know. New Zealand's notorious for coincidences.'

Long black lashes hid his eyes for a second. 'I hope not,' he said neutrally. 'But if it's inevitable, I certainly hope I see them before they see me. Have you come here for peace and solitude too?'

Ianthe turned her head to stare at the lake. Even through the thin cotton of her trousers she could feel the canvas squabs radiate the heat they'd trapped from the sun.

'Yes,' she said simply, for some reason no longer unwilling to talk about it. 'I got bitten by a shark, and when the whole media circus ended and I came out of hospital for the third time I just wanted to crawl away to heal by myself.'

If he'd shown any sign of pity she'd have set her glass down and made some excuse and left, but he said in a judicial voice, 'That must be the most terrifying thing that can happen to anyone.'

'Oddly enough, I don't think it was. I was half out of the water when it happened, climbing the ladder into the boat. I can't remember much, but I do recall thinking that I was in the shark's hunting grounds. And being surprised that there was no pain, although when it grabbed my leg I was shocked enough to punch it on the nose! I was lucky. It wasn't a big one, and apparently it didn't like being hit fair and square on its most sensitive spot.'

'What sort of shark?' he asked.

Surprised into laughter, because that was what her professor at university had asked when he'd come to see her in hospital, she told him, 'A Tiger Shark.'

'And did they catch it?'

She shook her head. 'No, they didn't try. Why kill something that's only doing what it was born to do? As far as we know—and in spite of *Jaws*—sharks don't turn into man-eaters, the way leopards or lions can. They just eat whatever comes to hand, and that day I was it.'

'You're remarkably tolerant,' he said, his tone oblique, almost cryptic. 'I'd be inclined to kill something that tried to eat me.'

After flicking him a glance, she became absorbed in the pattern of leaves on the ground. She believed him.

'They're an endangered species,' she said. 'I was in its element, and whenever you swim you risk bumping into something large and carnivorous or small and poisonous.'

'And you enjoy swimming.'

Ianthe drank some of the liquid, relishing the refreshing tartness. 'I always have,' she said at last.

His gaze sharpened, but after a moment he nodded. Feeling as a possum must when the spotlight swings away from its tree, Ianthe allowed herself to relax.

'You spoke of a media circus,' he said. 'Was that because you're a television celebrity?'

Mark, of course. It was unlikely *he'd* seen the documentary series—as far as she knew, it had only just sold to England and America. Wishing Mark had kept his mouth shut, Ianthe said lightly, 'Shark attacks are always newsworthy. I was only a very minor celebrity.' The scar on her leg itched. She ignored it, as she wished she could ignore Alex's speculative glance.

'And how did you get into such a career?' he asked.

He didn't sound avid, merely interested. Pleased at his restraint, Ianthe said, 'I'm a marine biologist, and I was working with dolphins in the Bay of Islands when a film crew thought I'd make a nice little clip on a reel they were making for Air New Zealand. About six months later someone rang up and asked if I'd front a documentary series about New Zealand's marine life.'

'And, dazzled by the glamour, you agreed.' His voice missed mockery by a whisker; although he was teasing her, there was understanding and amusement there.

She laughed. 'If that was the reason I'd have been very disappointed! We lived in pretty spartan conditions on a glorious schooner that was built for freight, not passengers. No, I decided to do it because I'd just had the plug pulled on my research funding and the film company offered good money—enough to keep me from going cap in hand to sponsors for quite a while if I lived economically.'

'And will you be going back to your dolphins?'

'As soon as I can.' She willed her face to reveal nothing, her eyes to remain cool and composed, willed him not to notice the guarded nature of her response.

She didn't know whether she'd succeeded.

Alex Considine didn't have a poker face, but she suspected he revealed only what he wanted to. At the moment he looked mildly interested.

'Did you enjoy the film work?'

'After a few initial hassles, yes.'

When he lifted his brows she explained drily, 'I didn't realise that all they expected was someone to look reasonable in a high-cut swimsuit, someone to frolic in the water. They wanted me to grow my hair so that I could flick it around for the camera, and they expected me to coo over lobsters and shells and pretty fish. After we'd sorted that out I liked it very much.'

'And how did you sort it out?' he asked, a smile tucking the corners of his controlled mouth.

'Got stroppy and waved my contract around a lot,' she said, 'until they realised that I actually did know what I was talking about and wasn't just some lightweight mermaid who was kinky enough to prefer dolphins to men.'

Enough bitterness seeped into her words for him to give

another of those laser glances. A shiver ran the length of her spine but she met his hooded eyes squarely.

'And do you prefer dolphins to men?' he asked, a lazy smile robbing the question of impertinence.

Ianthe laughed. 'You know where you are with dolphins,' she said, 'but, no, I don't.'

'Where are you with dolphins?'

'You're in their country, and you're a curiosity,' she said readily. She'd been talking far too much about herself, so she said, 'You've spent some time in England, I imagine, from your accent.'

He looked amused. 'My mother is the source of my accent. She has very strong opinions on the proper way to speak, and the ruthlessness to enforce them.'

'Persuading your children not to sound like some refugee from a cartoon is a never-ending business, I'm told,' Ianthe smiled as she thought of Tricia's battles with her five-year-old.

'I have no children,' he told her, his voice smooth and impersonal, 'but my friends certainly say so. I'm not married.'

He'd thought she was fishing. Fighting back her indignation, Ianthe tried to ignore the way her heart fluttered and soared.

He asked, 'Will you go back to working in television?'

'They don't want a front-person with a scar down her leg. It doesn't look good, and the limp is ungraceful.' Because it didn't matter, her voice was as pragmatic as her words.

She didn't quite hear what he said under his breath, but judging from the glitter in his eyes the succinct phrase was probably rude. Astonished, she looked up into a hard face and scornful, searing eyes.

'Did they tell you that?' he asked, on a note that sent a shiver up her spine.

'No, but it's the truth. Viewers don't like their programmes spoiled by ugly reminders that the real world has carnivores prowling it. People complain bitterly if they see insects eating each other on screen! Probably because most of us live in cities now we want to believe that the natural world is one of beauty and meaning and harmony.'

The harshness faded from his expression as he leaned back into his chair. 'But you don't believe that?'

She shrugged. 'It's extraordinarily beautiful, but it's also unsentimental. Animals kill and eat to survive. They're not pretty different-shaped humans with human attitudes. Even pack animals, which we can understand best, have a rigid hierarchy with crushing rules that would drive most of us insane.'

'But we're animals too.'

'Of course we are.' Made uneasy by the focused intentness of his gaze, Ianthe resisted the impulse to wriggle. 'Our problem is that we know what we're doing. Most animals live by instinct.'

'So it's not cruel for animals to drive an ill or wounded member from the pack, but humans shouldn't?'

For a moment she didn't realise what he meant. When she did she gave him a startled, angry glance. 'Animals drive their sick away or abandon them because their presence attracts predators. If you're using me as an instance, I'm not ill, but my wound could well have put an end to the series' existence if people had stopped watching. Besides, I was in hospital while they were filming the last programmes so they had to get someone to take my place. I have no hard feelings.'

'As I said before, you're astonishingly tolerant,' he said, his smile hard and humourless.

Oh, she could be enormously tolerant. The loss of her job was the least of her problems.

He said, 'Will you always have that limp?' He glanced at her trouser-clad leg.

For the first time Ianthe realised that most people when confronted with her scar did one of two things—the rude stared and commented while the polite kept their eyes fixed on her face. Both responses irritated her because they seemed to imply that she was less than perfect, less than human. Alex, however, looked at her leg without aversion.

'Always,' she said, steadying her voice so that her self-pity didn't show.

'You seem very relaxed about it.'

Although her unusual frankness had given him the opportunity to probe, she'd told him enough about herself. 'I try not to worry about things I can't control,' she said coolly. 'It doesn't always work, but fretting over the past is just a waste of time.'

'Fretting over anything is a waste of time.'

Nodding, she let the sun soak into her, acutely aware of the strumming of the cicadas, now reaching for a crescendo. However, balancing the shrill stridulation were other sounds—the soft rustling of reeds swaying against each other, the lazy cry of a gull that had drifted inland from the coast a few miles away, and the sound of a speedboat on the one lake that was open for powerboats, its intrusive roar muted by intervening hills to a pleasant hum.

And a fantail—the same one, perhaps?—black and cheeky as it darted around collecting insects from under the vine over the pergola.

Accepting her tacit refusal to discuss her leg any further, Alex Considine said, 'Do you know anything about the way dune lakes are formed? Why are there lakes in this valley, but not in the valleys on either side?'

'Because under this one there's an impermeable iron-stone pan. Rainwater collects above it and forms the lakes. The sand is silica, which is why it's so white.'

'So this is a rare formation?'

'No, there are similar lakes wherever there are sand-hills—on this coast they go right up to North Cape.'

He asked, 'Did you do geology at university also?'

'I'm just an interested amateur,' she said, getting up. 'I must go now. Thank you so much for the drink, and I hope your Range Rover is driveable soon.'

'It doesn't matter,' Alex said calmly, rising to tower over her. 'Mark isn't hurt and neither was anyone else; that's the important thing.'

Ianthe wanted to convince herself she was grateful that he didn't try to persuade her to stay. For all his exotic façade he was far too easy to talk to, and she'd revealed more about herself than she'd intended to. Much more than he'd told her about himself.

As they were going towards the front door Ianthe's leg failed her again. It was only a slight stumble, but Alex's hand shot out instantly, closing with hard strength onto her arm and supporting her. Ianthe had been stung by jellyfish; that was how she felt now—shock, and then a sensation like the thrust of a spear tempered on the edge of ice and fire.

Did he feel it too? She looked up, saw the beautiful mouth compress, harden.

'All right?' he asked abruptly, releasing her when he was sure she had regained her balance.

She managed to smile. 'Yes, thank you.'

'Do you need to rest?'

'No,' she said, adding with hasty firmness, 'And I don't need to be carried, either.'

He was frowning, the brilliant eyes resting on her leg. 'Will it always be likely to let you down?'

'No, they tell me it's going to be a lot better as soon as the muscles strengthen.'

Her surgeon had suggested she walk to build up the muscles, but she hadn't because she'd cringed at the idea of people pitying her as she limped by. Well, that very evening she'd begin exercising, and ignore the stares and whispered comments.

The decision buoyed her spirits. With erect back and shoulders she said goodbye and drove carefully down the drive, concentrating fiercely to stop the odd desolation that roiled inside her.

At the bach she pushed all the windows open before

going out onto the verandah overlooking the lake and collapsing into one of the elderly chairs to read the newspaper.

After ten minutes or so, she dropped it on the floor, feeling oddly detached, as though somehow she'd slipped through a transparent door and into another world.

The two men shaking hands on the front page weren't statesmen signing an important treaty; they were smirking actors chosen to fill empty space on the page. The people marching in the streets of the capital city in a tiny state somewhere on the Adriatic Sea were extras from an old movie, selected for their lined, worn faces and dressed by Wardrobe in thick, drab peasants' clothing.

Only the photograph of children playing in the sea meant anything; yes, she thought, looking at them with her heart compressed into a painful knot, they were real, they were complete and oh, they were lucky.

To break the soggy spell of self-pity, she strode over the thick, springy kikuyu grass to the edge of the busy beach. Small children ran around happily, yelling and laughing, many swam in the milky band of water that denoted the shallows.

Ianthe closed her eyes but immediately forced her lashes back up. Beneath her breath she muttered, 'I'm not going to stand here like a wimp,' and walked across the blinding white sand.

Nausea clutched her before she'd gone halfway. Breathing shallowly, fighting back the panic that turned her clammy and shaking, she forced herself to stand there for long, chilling moments before turning and stumbling back.

A couple of youths were passing; through the roaring in her ears she heard one jeer, 'Hey, blondie, need some help?'

Intent only on reaching sanctuary, she blundered past. His companion said something and followed it up by catching her arm.

A voice cracked out across the beach. 'Let her go.'

They swivelled around, both assuming the swaggering,

aggressive posture of a male whose territory has been violated. Heart thudding painfully in her throat, Ianthe froze.

Alex Considine was taller than they were, but they were stocky, tight-skinned and muscular, with necks wider than their heads, their macho strut a violent contrast to his athletic grace. Yet such was the dark power of Alex's personality that after one glance the man who held Ianthe dropped her arm as though her skin burned his fingers, and the other said uneasily, 'She's OK, mate. We thought she was going to fall over,' before stepping back and decamping.

Alex didn't even watch them go. 'Are you all right?' he demanded as he closed the gap between them with a couple of long strides. His hands fastened onto her, holding her up by her shoulders, and for a paralysing moment she was exposed to the full intensity of his gaze.

Ianthe knew she had skin the colour of cottage cheese and dark blotches under her eyes. She swallowed to ease her dry mouth, but could only croak, 'Yes.'

Alex's quiet, 'What the hell is the matter with you?' made her stomach leap.

She dragged in a deep, shuddering breath. 'I'm sorry,' she said stupidly, trying to overcome the empty sickness of fear.

He said, 'Come on,' and turned her towards the bach. A steel-hard arm buttressed her, giving her the strength to climb the low bank. 'We'll go inside,' he said, his voice oddly distant.

Numbly she obeyed the crisp command and crossed the wide back verandah, where chairs sat in shabby communion. As they passed the low table he picked up a plastic bag.

'What are you doing here?' Ianthe asked woodenly after he'd pushed the door open and let her go through.

'You forgot your frozen goods.' Without asking permission he put the bag into her small freezer compartment. 'You need some stimulant. I'll make coffee.'

She clenched her jaw to keep her teeth from chattering. 'I don't want anything, thanks. I'm fine now.'

Ignoring her, he opened the door into the fridge and removed a jug of orange juice. 'This will do,' he said, pouring a glass and bringing it across to her. 'Sit down,' he ordered, his unwavering gaze commanding her obedience.

It was too much trouble to protest, so she collapsed ungracefully into a chair. He waited until she'd pushed the heavy, clinging hair back from her face, then offered the glass. Accepting it, Ianthe watched with outrage and dismay as it wobbled in her hand.

'I'll do it,' Alex Considine said abruptly, and took it back, holding it to her mouth so that she could sip the sweetly tart liquid.

It helped. Soon she felt secure enough to take the glass and gulp down more of the juice.

He waited until she'd almost finished before asking evenly, 'What happened? What did they say to you?'

'It wasn't them.' She dismissed the two men.

'Then what?'

His level voice didn't fool her; she wasn't going to be able to fob him off. Ianthe bent her head so that she couldn't see the narrow masculine hips, the long muscular legs. The silence hummed, strident with the confusion in her head, in her heart.

Eventually she said, 'I had a dizzy turn.'

Although he said nothing, his disbelief was patent.

Slowly she finished the juice. 'Thank you,' she said, her throat thick.

'Look at me,' he ordered.

Lifting her chin was a mistake, and staring him full in the eyes, daring him to take the issue any further, was an even bigger one. Alex's pale gaze drilled through her meagre defences.

'Have you got sunstroke?' he asked.

It would have been a pat answer, but she shook her head. Lies didn't come easily to her. 'No. I just felt a bit—overwhelmed.' She couldn't breathe in the hot room and her skin was too sensitive, too tight. 'I think I'd rather be outside,' she said, forcing her voice into something like normality. 'It's cooler on the verandah.'

'All right. Do you need help?'

'No!' She tried to soften the blunt refusal. 'I feel much better now.'

But once outside she realised she needed activity to burn off the adrenalin that still pumped through her body. Looking towards the motor camp, she asked aggressively, 'Would you like to go for a walk and see how the other half spend their holidays?'

With a keen look he answered crisply, 'Why not?'

Nothing had changed. Children, hatted and slick with sunscreen, still laughed and called in clear, high voices, still splashed in the chalky water that stretched out to where the lake bed dropped away.

The edge was still as sharp and sudden against the fierce, glinting blue of the deeper water.

Ianthe averted her eyes and concentrated hard on walking through the holidaymakers without giving away how aware she was of the man who strode beside her. Sand crunched beneath their feet. Alex looked around, the fan of wrinkles at the corners of his eyes slightly indented. How old was he? Thirty-three or four, she guessed.

He said, 'This place reminds me of the village I lived in until I was ten.'

Intrigued, Ianthe was stopped from asking questions by an indefinable reserve in his tone, in the angular, aristocratic line of his profile.

They walked around families, past groups of teenagers indulging in their noisy, unsophisticated courtship rituals, and as they went by Ianthe felt the eyes, some on her, some on Alex. She was accustomed to being watched; it interested her that Alex too had developed a way to deal with onlookers. He didn't make eye contact, he walked steadily—not fast, not slow—and although he swivelled when a child shrieked behind them he turned away again immediately he realised it was under supervision.

Who was he? She recognised his name, so possibly he had turned up in a newspaper. However, she had a strongly visual memory; if she'd seen a photograph of him she'd have remembered his startling good looks and pale eyes instead of merely being haunted by a vague familiarity.

Yet would any photograph capture the magnetism of his personality, or the aura of uncompromising authority?

Probably not, and she wasn't going to think about it any more. That way lay danger.

Although she'd snatched up a straw hat as they left the bach, the sun beat down on her shoulders and summoned a rare blue sheen from Alex's bare head. She should tell him he needed some protection, but it seemed an oddly personal and intimate thing to talk about.

'You obviously know this place very well,' Alex commented.

Nodding, she kept her eyes on the low bushes—a mixture of sedges, rushes and sprawling teatree—that scrambled from the pine plantation to the water, effectively marking the limit of the beach. 'For years I spent every school holiday here with my best friend. Her parents own the bach.'

Once she'd known every inch of the shoreline. In those long, golden, distant summers she and Tricia had spent every day on or in the lake. And now Tricia was a wife and mother, and Ianthe was trying to reassemble her life.

'We'd better go back,' she said evenly. 'It's swampy in there.' She glanced down at his feet and added with a spark of malice, 'You won't want to get those shoes wet.'

He laughed softly. 'I'd noticed that I was overdressed,' he said, turning the tables neatly on her.

Biting her lip, she swivelled, and of course her wretched leg chose just that moment to let her down again. Gasping, she jerked back, but too late. Her sideways lurch had thrown her into the tangle of bushes, and her foot sank into the lake so that water rose halfway up her calf.

Panic, sickening and immediate, clawed at her. For a horrifying second she couldn't move, until the clamouring terror forced her free of the water. Whimpering, she pushed past Alex, blundering across the hot sand in a desperate rush to reach the safety of solid ground.

CHAPTER THREE

SHE was almost there when hard hands caught her, gripping her cruelly until she stopped fighting and went limp against him, panic giving way to a shamed exhaustion.

'All right,' Alex said quietly. 'It's all right, Ianthe. You're safe.'

'I know,' she choked, trying to pull away, because it was too easy to surrender mindlessly to his disciplined toughness.

A simple offer of comfort, she told her hammering heart, that was all it was. He'd given her the only things she could take any consolation from—the tempered support of his body, the knowledge that she wasn't alone.

Swiftly he turned, forcing her around so that his broad shoulders sheltered her from any curious stares, then let her go. A quick glance informed her that no one had noticed, and some of the tight knot of humiliation eased.

But when she looked back at Alex she couldn't escape those enigmatic eyes, eyes that goaded her into muttering, 'Don't you pity me.'

Something predatory prowled through the icy depths. 'Pity you?' His smile was taut and compelling. 'I don't pity you, Ianthe Brown. Far from it.' Strong fingers bit into her arm, turned her, tucked her hand in the crook of his elbow. 'All right, we'll walk back in the shade of the trees. What birds do you usually see on the lakes?'

Ianthe forced herself to respond. 'Dotterels nest in scrapes in the sand, and in spring and autumn the lakes are a staging point for migratory birds.' As she answered his questions her voice sounded flat and dull, but by the time

43

they got back to the bach the black panic had withdrawn into its lurking limbo on the borders of her mind.

She said, 'I'd like to sit outside.'

He waited until she'd chosen a shabby, comfortable chair, then leaned against the railing and looked down at her. Without preamble he commanded, 'Tell me why a woman who's terrified of the water should choose to stay no more than twenty-five metres away from it.'

She owed him an explanation, but all she could say was a muted, 'I just have to get used to it again.'

His scrutiny pierced her fragile shell of composure, splintering it into shards. At the end of the most tense silence Ianthe had ever endured, he asked, 'Haven't you been able to go in the water since the shark attacked you?'

'No.' Her voice was hoarse. She cleared her throat and went on, 'It's not the water. It's teeth. I dream of dolphins, and they play and smile, and then their smiles turn into teeth and—and—I'm terrified something will catch me and drag me down, and that this time I'll die.'

'Ianthe,' he said deeply, and came across and sat down beside her, took her tense hand in his strong, warm one.

Something snapped inside her. Hastily, indistinctly, she muttered, 'I'm not scared of water—I can wallow in a bath and clean my teeth without flinching, drive across the Harbour Bridge without turning a hair, even walking along the beach is all right. But if I—well, you saw.'

'So you came *here* to get over it?'

Ianthe shivered at the savage irony of his tone. With eyes fixed on the vivid cobalt surface of the lake she said, 'This is where I learned to swim. Tricia and I splashed around in the shallows, then her mother taught us the strokes and jollied us into swimming properly. It seemed the most natural thing in the world—and so utterly safe. That first summer she wouldn't let us swim through the wall—it was out there in front of us, tantalising and forbidden. Do you know what I mean?'

'By the wall? I presume it's the drop-off into deeper

water. I'd noticed it—it's unusually obvious.' He spoke with a cool intonation, as though measuring every word he said.

'The bed of the lake is actually below sea level. That depth and the extreme clarity of the water and the brilliant whiteness of the sand all combine to make the wall.' Keeping her head averted, she eased her hand away from his grip. Her pulses thudded through the fragile veins at her wrist and she looked at his hand, lean-fingered and competent.

But not relaxed, she thought with a bleak surprise. No, there was tension in those tanned fingers and she could feel it crackle around her. Not that she blamed him; she was probably embarrassing him horribly. No doubt he couldn't get away fast enough.

Straightening her back, she stared blindly across the verandah and went on, 'Swimming through it is like breaking through a barrier, free-falling into another dimension. However often I did it I always loved it, that moment when I burst through into the blue. I felt strong and different, the sort of person who could do anything.'

'You *are* the sort of person who can do anything,' he said curtly. 'This is temporary, a normal response to the trauma of pain and shock and terror.'

Anger ricocheted through her, hot and sudden and fierce. 'I can't even put my feet into the water! I'd hoped that coming here would help—after all, the biggest wildlife in this water are eels.' Her voice bit sardonically into the words. 'And they're not noted for ferocious attacks on human beings.'

'So it hasn't worked yet. Give it time, and it will.' He got to his feet and walked across to the rail, leaning against it to look over the lake.

Numbly Ianthe watched the muscles of his thighs flex, the lithe grace as he moved. 'I'm beginning to wonder,' she said bleakly. 'You saw me when I tripped. It's called a panic attack.'

'You expect too much, too soon. Have you had any counselling?'

She shook her head. 'Apart from Tricia, I haven't told anyone else but you.'

'Why?'

She heard the frown in his tone. Clasping her hands in her lap, she concentrated on the way the sun fell across them, emphasising thin fingers and pale skin.

Slowly she said, 'Because I feel—reduced, I suppose. And I didn't understand how bad it was until I came here. I'm fine in swimming pools, and although I knew the sea made me panicky I didn't realise why. I thought I just needed to take things quietly and I'd be all right in no time.'

He turned his head so that he was looking at her, eyes burning like pale flames in the darkness of his face. 'You shouldn't be alone. Where is your family?'

That tantalising hint of an alien accent, an unknown language, lingered in his autocratic voice. 'My mother's dead,' she told him, fighting off an enormous lassitude that rolled over her, sapping her strength, loosening her tongue. 'My father is busy with his second wife and second family. Anyway, I don't need anyone—what could they do?' She lifted weighted lashes and managed to curve her lips into an approximation of a smile. 'Actually, today was quite a step forward. I was in the water for a fraction of a second and didn't—quite—succumb to hysterics.'

'I saw how much it cost you,' Alex said tersely. 'You need help for this, not solitude and will-power. Is there no one who can come and stay with you? This Tricia—your friend? Surely—?'

'No, she's got a husband and two small children, and her own life to lead.' Ianthe covered a yawn with a boneless hand. 'I'm sorry, I'm really tired.'

'Then go inside and sleep,' he ordered, his tone almost impatient.

She stumbled when she got to her feet, prepared this time

for the lean hand on her arm that steadied her. 'Sorry,' she repeated.

'Why? Because you tried to stay in the water in spite of what it cost you mentally and emotionally? It was foolish, perhaps, but admirable. Will you be all right by yourself? I'll stay if you want me to.'

'No!' She saw his eyes darken and stepped away. 'No, I'm fine. It just takes it out of me...' Will-power finally fastened her lips on the gabbling words.

Silence, heavy and punishing, held her in stasis. She didn't look at him, but her eyes caught a muscle flicking against the angular line of his jaw.

Then he said, 'All right. Don't go back into the water again.'

Did he really think he could toss orders around and expect her to obey them? 'Chance,' she said, breathing rapidly, 'would be a fine thing.'

He made her lock the front and back door; when he'd gone she sat down and waited until she heard a vehicle drive away. Then she staggered into the bedroom, where she dropped onto the narrow bed and went gratefully to sleep.

To dream of dolphins, sleek and sinuous, graceful and strong and mysterious, with eyes the colour of the sea at twilight, and she struggled to cry out, because she knew what was going to happen.

But as she swam with them one turned into a merman. He took her hand and pulled her down into the water, and when she panicked he laughed, and those eyes held her prisoner, and they went down and down and down, so that she stopped struggling and drowned in those pale, translucent eyes...

Somehow she realised he was naked, and so was she, and she shivered as the water rippled across her body, sleek as silk, cool and tempting, but not as tempting as the merman, who kissed her, not as sleek as his powerful muscles and tanned skin, not as terrifying as his passionate mouth and the heated darkness of her own response.

When she woke she stretched her aching body and thought wryly that she didn't have to search far for the meaning of that dream. A languorous shiver moved slowly through her. Held captive by the keen needle of unfulfilled hunger at the heart of her drowsiness, she couldn't break free of the aftermath. Such an instant attraction had never happened to her before, but she'd seen and heard enough of the 'eyes meeting across a crowded room' syndrome to accept that it wasn't uncommon.

Alex hadn't shown any signs of reciprocating. But then, would she recognise them? She'd been very careful to hide her own response, and his self-possession was far more seamless than hers. Whoever he was, and whatever he did, very few thoughts or emotions escaped the lean, fine-featured face, those piercing eyes, that well-defined mouth.

For a while she lay, letting her lax body gradually cool, the heat die, until sluggishly she looked at her watch. Five-forty-five. And at that moment, as she thought longingly of a shower, she remembered where she'd seen the name Alex Considine before.

In the business pages of a newspaper, when she'd been recovering from the operation that had pinned the two pieces of her leg back together. Reclusive Alex Considine, billionaire Alex Considine, who'd started with nothing at secondary school and before he'd got his first degree had built a computer software fortune that had just kept growing because he was the best at what he did.

His name, the memory of that article, the photograph that had accompanied it buzzed through her brain, and she realised just how much she'd allowed herself to fantasise about him. Quickly she got to her feet and showered in cold water, telling herself that the shock was good for her. Then she switched on the television and watched the news with desperate concentration.

Three people had died on Mount Cook, New Zealand's

highest mountain, another two had drowned off one of the West Coast beaches. A blizzard was ravaging the east coast of North America, snow blanketed Europe, and a plane had crashed in Africa.

And the protesters still walked the streets of their small city somewhere on the Adriatic Sea. Rank upon rank of them, line upon line, spilling through the narrow lanes, debouching onto wider, tree-lined boulevards, their dark, bony faces filled with a kind of fierce exultation. They looked cold and poor and determined.

'...for the third week in succession,' the journalist said, speaking rapidly at the camera. 'So far there has been no violence—' the camera switched to a uniformed man, glum and silent on the side of the road— 'but the ruling regime has used force against the Illyrians before, and many of these marchers consider it only a matter of time before blood flows once more in these streets.'

Ianthe switched the set off and went to cook dinner.

So Alex Considine inhabited the world of the very rich. Well, she'd known that right from the beginning. The house had told her, and so had his sophistication.

Therefore was no need for this—this stupid *anguish*. She wanted him, but she could overcome that. Her undisciplined body would soon forget, because she wouldn't be seeing him again.

And she had other things to think of. She'd made a start, she thought sturdily. She'd actually stood in the water. Oh, it had been accidental, and she'd just about passed out with terror, but for a few seconds her foot had been under the water.

Tomorrow she'd do it again, deliberately this time, and eventually she'd be able to stand in the lake without that hideous panic clogging her brain, and when she could do that the worst would be over. She'd go back into the ocean without fearing a terror from beneath the waters, a terror that carried blood and pain and a hideous death in its jaws.

Perhaps because she'd slept so heavily during the day

she couldn't settle after dinner. When the last of the sun's light had seeped from behind the hills she stared from the window at a sky so thickly encrusted with stars that it looked like a celestial city. The lake's surface gleamed dark as obsidian. Ianthe gave in to her restlessness and went for a walk along the beach.

A week before Christmas the first cyclone had freshened the countryside, so now, instead of the hot, dry scent of hay, the damp air carried the heavy perfume of growing vegetation. Even the crisp pine balsam had no effect against that elemental lushness. It tugged at Ianthe's body, teasing nerve-ends, beckoning, luring her out onto the coolly glimmering sand, whispering of secret delights and hidden, guilty pleasures.

'Oh, for heaven's sake!' she said out loud.

This was lust, consuming but uncomplicated, the straightforward, animal urge to procreate; he was an alpha male and she a fertile woman—just what Mother Nature ordered for the continuation of the species.

However, she told herself, moving unsteadily across the crisp, ghost-white sand, he's not likely to be attracted to a woman with an ugly scar on one leg, a woman who limps so ungracefully that she can't dance and can't run. He could have any woman in the world—even if he weren't amazingly, appallingly rich.

Her leg began to ache. Taking the weight off the strained muscles, she leaned against the bole of a tree for several minutes before beginning the walk back. Getting fit was important, but she'd have to be careful not to overdo it.

A hundred metres or so from the bach she stiffened, wary as a cat when the hint of a threat impinged on its acute senses. Almost instantly the fundamental fear gave way to something else, for she recognised the man who stood at the edge of the lake, a tall figure cloaked in starshine and darkness, and it was anticipation that thudded in her throat and beat on wings through her body.

He didn't speak and neither did she. Together they

walked up to the verandah. Neither sat, however. They stood a few feet apart, taut, like antagonists waiting to see who would give in first.

Alex said curtly, 'I had to know you were all right.'

'Of course I'm all right.'

'So you are.' His voice was hard.

Ianthe's heart beat high in her throat. If he'd stayed away she'd never have seen him again. She knew that, just as she knew to a centimetre how long the scar on her leg was. Perhaps he too was aware that his return had opened a door both of them preferred to keep closed.

Somehow she had to retreat through that door and close it firmly behind her, barring the siren lure of passion. She didn't indulge in brief romances—especially with men like Alex Considine.

But oh, it was difficult to say briskly, 'It's very kind of you to come, but really you didn't need to. I'm fine.'

Her eyes were so adapted to the night that she saw the unsettling smile he gave her, caught the glitter of his eyes before the dark lashes hid them.

'I'm not a particularly kind person,' he said. 'It was a quixotic impulse.'

'As quixotic as not telling me who you are?' she snapped.

He knew immediately what she meant. His face hardened and his eyes narrowed, giving him a hooded, dangerous look. 'Are you a snob, Ianthe?'

'No.' She couldn't tell him that his silence had seemed like a small betrayal.

'Then what difference does it make what I do for a living?'

None to him, certainly. And none, she thought, firming her lips, to her, either. 'I suppose it's difficult to tell people that you're a software king.'

'It's not important,' he said abruptly, watching her keenly.

And no, it wasn't, except that it had shattered a few dreams she hadn't even been aware of harbouring.

'I don't suppose it is,' she said, wishing now that she'd had the sense to shut up.

'So are we still friends?'

Had they been friends? No, her body said. Friendship was the last thing she wanted from him. Yes, her mind contradicted, there had been the beginnings of a tenuous friendship there, because nothing else was possible.

'Of course,' she said brightly.

A rough undernote gave force to his quiet laughter. 'Then I won't outstay my welcome,' he said. 'Goodnight, Ianthe.'

'Goodnight.'

Immobile, her body aching with unwanted need, Ianthe forced herself to stay on the porch until his car purred away. Why had he come? That sense of responsibility, of course. He'd needed to see for himself that she'd recovered from her involuntary step into the water, and now, duty done, he'd gone, and she'd never see him again.

Yes, that had to be it. Any other idea was too dangerous to consider.

Shivering, her leg throbbing, she limped into the bach and locked the door behind her as though shutting out some feral creature of the night.

'Are you stocking up for the cyclone?' the woman behind the counter said, ringing up the charges.

Frowning, Ianthe asked, 'What cyclone? We've only just had one—'

'Haven't you heard? On the news this morning they said that another one—possibly much stronger than the ones before Christmas—is brewing up in the Coral Sea.'

'We've never had three in one year before!'

'Global warming, I suppose.' She looked gloomy, as well she might. Cyclones were not good for business. 'Or, as my grandson says, global warning.'

'They're only cyclonic storms when they get to New Zealand,' Ianthe comforted, 'and they usually go down the east coast, so we're on the sheltered side here.'

After saying goodbye, she scooped up her groceries and left the store. Outside the sun dazzled on the water from a sky as blue and bold as a cornflower; already hot, it was getting hotter. A cyclone seemed unlikely.

Perhaps she should stock up with extra food—but cyclones were notoriously erratic and her fridge was small. She'd have plenty of time to shop if it decided to head towards Northland.

When she got home, she thought, she'd walk down to the water and stand with her feet in it—no, perhaps she should do it here, where the children played and chased each other and splashed. Clutching the plastic bag of groceries, she limped across the sand.

It took so much will-power to walk to the edge—to stand with her feet six inches from the water—that a grey dizziness threatened to bring her to her knees. Grimly, her throat and mouth dry, her heart labouring, she stood there with the sun battering her head, then stooped, wrenched off her sandals, and dropped them beside the groceries. Straightening, she dragged in a deep, harsh breath and took the final step.

Water oozed over her toes, licked along the soles of her feet, climbed halfway to her ankles. Wildness beat up through her, clamoured at the gates of her will, swamped her so that she was going to scream...

Repressing the frantic instinct to run, she jerked backwards out of the inch-deep water and forced herself to turn and walk.

One, she thought doggedly. Two. Two steps—that's all you need to go. Now stop. Right here.

Her lungs fought for breath; gasping, hyperventilating, she wondered if anything was worth this torment. After all, she could stay away from the sea for the rest of her life...

A girl of about five came dancing up—big dark eyes,

hair the colour of a burnished chestnut, skin glistening with sunscreen. 'You should have a hat on,' she said, her stern little voice breaking into Ianthe's absorption.

Ianthe swallowed. 'I know,' she said huskily.

'My mum says, "Don't ever go out without a hat."'

'Your mum is right,' Ianthe agreed.

'Have you got a hat?'

'Yes, I have. A big straw one with a flower on it.' Her heart was slowing, the sick terror fading, her breath returning to its normal even pace.

'It's no use in the car,' the girl said, clearly parroting her mother. 'It won't stop you getting burned if you leave it there.'

Ianthe threw her a suitably chastened look. 'How about if I promise not ever to come outside again without my hat and sunscreen on?' she asked.

'Make sure you don't,' her new acquaintance chided, clapping a hand over her mouth to hide her grin.

It overflowed, and Ianthe's laughter joined the girl's.

Sobering abruptly, the child said, 'Oh, you've got a sore leg. What did you do to it?'

'I cut it on something very sharp.'

'It looks *sore*!'

A tightening between her shoulderblades brought Ianthe's head around, her smile dying as a car pulled up on the road close by and a man said smoothly, 'Ianthe.'

'Do you know him?' the girl asked, staring at Alex.

He got out, lean and dynamic in his well-cut clothes, sunglasses hiding those amazing eyes.

'Yes,' Ianthe said, wishing she'd gone straight home, wishing this delightful child hadn't sidetracked her. She'd have been safe now, instead of standing there while Alex walked with lithe masculine grace towards her.

'My mum says I shouldn't get into cars with strangers,' the child said, made uneasy, perhaps, by the sizzle of tension in the atmosphere.

'Your mum's quite right,' Alex said, and smiled. 'Don't

ever get into a car with a stranger. But I'm not going to offer you a lift, and Ianthe is a friend of mine.'

Ianthe's heart bumped, and adrenalin from a different source began to flow through her body.

With resignation she watched the girl succumb to that blazing charm. Giving him her brilliant beam, she said, 'She hasn't got a hat on, and neither have you.'

'I won't be out of my car for long,' Alex said, 'and from now on Ianthe will make sure she takes a hat with her wherever she goes.'

He hadn't looked at her; all his attention was on the child, who preened a little and asked, 'Are you going to give her a ride? She's got a sore leg. You should kiss it better. My mum always—'

'Cleome! Cleome, come here!'

The girl said, 'That's my mum. I have to go. Goodbye.' She smiled at them both and ran off across the white sand, enviably light, enviably free from the burdens of adulthood.

After a swift glance at Ianthe's face, Alex said harshly, 'She's only a child—'

'I don't mind children,' Ianthe interrupted. 'They're honest and straightforward and they really want to know. What I hate is *pity*. People who feel sorry for me are really saying that a scar is going to mark me for life, change everything, reduce me to a lesser person. I refuse to be pitied.' She spat the last word out before realising, hot with embarrassment, that she'd spoken rapidly, fiercely, anger erupting from nowhere.

Alex's sunglasses were so dark she couldn't make out his eyes, but he was watching her intently, his mouth curved in an odd, humourless smile. 'I don't pity you,' he said.

Awkwardly Ianthe responded, 'I didn't mean to harangue you. My leg is going to be all right after I've had another op and worked on the muscles to strengthen them. It's just that I've been on the end of so much shocked sympathy that I tend to get a bit carried away. I'm sorry.'

'I tend to get carried away too,' he said, but ironically, as though there was some hidden meaning to the comment. 'Did you walk down?'

'Yes.'

'Do you want a lift back?'

'That would be great.'

If she was really serious about exercising her leg she'd walk, but the road was dusty and potholed and she was tired, although the overwhelming tiredness that hit each time she confronted her panic had been driven away by Alex's arrival. Cynically she told herself to stop making excuses; this coincidental meeting would probably be the last time she saw him. She had no intention of following up on their acquaintance, and it was very unlikely he'd come looking for her.

While he picked up her groceries she wiped the clinging grains of sand from her skin and slid into her sandals. Just as they reached his car she remembered what the shop-keeper had said. 'Did you know there's supposed to be another cyclone coming?'

Frowning, he nodded. 'Didn't you?'

'No.'

'Don't you watch television or listen to the radio?'

She shrugged. 'Some television,' she admitted. 'But I've been turning it off before the weather forecast.'

'From now on it might pay to keep an eye on it,' he said austerely, and opened the door for her. 'Ianthe,' he said when she was halfway in.

The amusement in his tone feathered across her nerves. 'What?'

'Next time you go outside, make sure you wear your hat.'

Her laugh was uneven. 'She's a darling, isn't she?' Settling into the seat, she did up the belt while he put the grocery bag in the rear.

Once beside her, he inserted the key into the ignition.

Without turning it, he said, 'I saw you in the water. Are you all right?'

'I'm fine. It wasn't easy, and I was shivering a bit when I got out, but Cleome soon chased that away.'

He gave her a hard look. 'You're still as white as a lily,' he said. 'Have lunch with me.'

Any sensible person would say no. But, after all, what harm could it possibly do? Lunch with an interesting man was not high on her list of dangers to avoid, even if he was a billionaire. Knowing that for the sake of her future peace of mind she should refuse, Ianthe said, 'I'd like that very much.'

'Good,' he said, and switched on the engine. The car hummed into life and he did a U-turn.

'I should change,' she said.

'You're fine the way you are.'

Her tan shirt and faded shorts suited her, but the clothes themselves were old; only their supreme comfort kept them in her wardrobe. If his house was any indication he liked cool, sophisticated elegance, and odds were, she thought glumly, that was the sort of woman he enjoyed—women who dressed as fastidiously as he did, beautiful women, with an eye for style and understated chicness.

So he'd invited her not out of pity, but because that strong sense of responsibility drove him. And she'd accepted because he made her feel alive again.

Ten minutes later she was revelling in the serenity, the cool, calm ambience, of Alex Considine's house. He was the most intriguing man she'd ever met, and because she wasn't going to succumb to this feverish, helpless fascination she could enjoy the time she spent with him and then go on her way without any regrets.

There'd be no bones broken, she thought, and recalled notices she'd seen in beauty spots. *Take nothing but photographs, leave nothing but footprints.* That was how it would be; she'd take only pleasant memories, and leave the same behind her.

They ate out on the terrace at a glass table. The meal was good—salads, she recalled later, when it was important to remember every second of that day. But although she enjoyed the food it was just generic, tasty and well-prepared as it was.

Like a squirrel she stored memories—every expression on Alex's dark, clever face as they talked of many things: books, the future of the Internet, their favourite foods, where the world was heading, the latest theory on the extinction of the dinosaurs, laughing as they swapped more and more outrageous reasons for the fact that miniskirts were only popular in times of prosperity.

His keen, swift brain stretched hers. She loved the way he laughed, loved making him laugh. He asked her more about her career and she spoke passionately about it, pleased because his questions and comments were astute and penetrating.

Stealthily, Ianthe watched the way the sun warmed his bronzed skin, outlining him in bold relief. He had, she thought as they drank coffee in silent harmony, a face that belonged to legends; the sculpted features were stamped with the authority and unyielding male beauty attributed to heroes and princes. It was the kind of face that stared from old paintings and medieval manuscripts—masterful, determined, imbued with a sense of destiny.

Men like him, sword in hand and clad in armour or the rich robes of privilege, had cut their way through the centuries. Robber barons who'd come from nowhere, yet with a combination of brute force, intelligence and that indefinable quality called leadership had forged destinies for themselves.

Somehow his reticence was appropriate. A man of mystery, she thought ironically, trying to wake herself from her dangerous mood. She was abandoning her common sense to a perilous fantasy about a dark knight.

'Would you like to go for a walk?' he asked lazily, his voice smoky and deep in the still, humid air.

Ianthe seized the idea gratefully. 'As long as we keep to the shade of the trees.'

'We could go down to the water for a few minutes,' he suggested, watching her from half-closed eyes.

Ianthe tensed. 'All right,' she said after a moment, ashamed of the wobble in her voice.

He didn't touch her as they walked to the edge of the lake, as she slipped her sandals off and set her teeth and looked at the water, transparent against the gleaming, burnished sand. No wind ruffled the surface so no wavelets could sneak up on her

Steeling herself, Ianthe took a minuscule step forward.

'Relax,' Alex said from beside her.

'That's easy to say.' But because he stood so close her mind was no longer obsessively fixated on her shallow heartbeat and rising dread.

He reached out and took her hand, and as the power of his touch poured through her like liquid lightning she took that final step and stood with her toes in the water, staring blindly out across the kingfisher surface, fighting back nausea and the clammy chill of panic.

'You've got guts, Ianthe,' he said, and let go her hand, ignoring the way her fingers clutched at his.

'Hardly.' Her voice trembled but she stayed there, the calm water barely wetting her feet. She dragged in a deep, gasping breath, but beneath it she felt a tiny thrill of relief because she was able to bear it.

'Oh, yes. You've endured what must be one of the worst experiences that can happen to a human being and you're determined to overcome it. That takes courage.'

She took another two or three short breaths, and he said sharply, 'Hyperventilating won't help.'

'I'm not hyperventilating.' Her voice sounded perfectly normal, and between her surprise at that and the need to explain, the dark apprehension lightened a fraction. 'It's a breathing exercise.'

'Does it help?'

Her lips stretched in a mockery of a smile. 'I'm not running screaming from the water, so it must.'

But as though the words had snapped the thin string of her control she turned and blundered out and away from that smiling, warm intensity of blue and stood shaking, staring sightlessly at the thrumming green of the pines as the sand burned the soles of her feet.

Harshly Alex said, 'God, I'm sorry—arrogantly, I thought perhaps my presence might make it easier.' And he picked her up in one smooth, astonishingly powerful movement and carried her into the black-green shade of the trees.

She staggered when he set her on her feet and he snatched her upright. Ianthe clutched at him, feeling beneath acutely sensitised fingers the swift bunch and coil of his muscles through the thin cotton of his shirt.

For heart-shaking moments they stood together, her breasts crushed against the wide wall of his chest. Shatteringly, the black fear receded, and she became acutely aware of the strength of the arms around her and the subtle, heated scent of him—not musky, exactly, but wholly, sensuously male...

Aware too of the press of lean hips and heavily muscled thighs, the male signals of arousal, imperative and elemental. In a primal response to that erotic stimulus her bones liquefied as heat flared in the hidden parts of her body, acute and consuming, rendering her pliable and yearning.

'It's all right,' he said, the words deep and sensuous and quiet. 'Ianthe, it's all right...'

His mouth touched her forehead in a gesture meant to comfort, then moved lightly across to a vulnerable temple and lingered. Her breath stopped in her throat. Poised on the edge of surrender, she waited.

And then an instinct as old as self-preservation shouted a warning. Rejecting the fierce, perilous urgency gathering inside her, she pulled away. His arms tightened for a second, then released her. Face averted, she took a couple of steps backwards into safety.

'Sorry,' she said huskily, because it was all she could think of.

'*I'm* sorry.' Anger burned beneath the controlled words. 'I shouldn't have persuaded you to go in.'

She glanced at him, her gaze stripped of everything but naked honesty, forcing herself to meet the turbulent, crystalline eyes. 'You didn't persuade me. I have to do it,' she said starkly. 'If I don't get over this I'm not ever going to be able to work again. At least I didn't feel sick this time. That's progress.'

Some primitive part of Ianthe rejoiced at the effort it took to banish the savage glitter from his eyes, and resented the irony of the smile that replaced it.

'It is indeed,' he said, and together they walked back beneath the trees to the house.

Mark was waiting for them, his expression not changing when Alex asked abruptly, 'What is it?'

'A telephone call, sir.'

'I'll take it in the office.'

'Yes, sir.' As Mark turned to go Alex said, 'Get Miss Brown a drink, please.'

'No, thanks, I don't need one.' Ianthe knew her voice was stiff, but she felt fragile and edgy and she didn't want Mark, who was probably a bodyguard, bringing her anything.

Alex gave her a keen look, then nodded and left with Mark, clearly dismissing her from his mind as Mark said something in a low voice. They were still close enough for her to see the way Alex's shoulders stiffened.

Hell, she thought, huddling into the cool embrace of a wicker chair. Oh, hell, what had happened in those moments she'd spent in his arms? Somehow her world had fundamentally shifted, a change as dramatic and shattering as if the poles had reversed themselves so that what used to be north was now south.

CHAPTER FOUR

STARING at the expensive table in front of her, the disciplined, chaste beauty of the room, she told herself fiercely it couldn't be love, because love came slowly, with understanding. Ianthe knew about love, had tasted its delights, remembered how shattered she'd been when it was snatched away. This overwhelming, feverish hunger—so consuming that she felt like a bundle of exposed nerve-ends—was sexual desire, that most primitive and wayward of needs after breathing and eating.

All right, she thought, yawning as she strove to strip her bewildering complexity of emotions back to the basic bedrock; all right, she wanted to make love with Alex Considine. Had, in fact, since the first time she'd seen him.

It was a simple response to a simple situation. Nothing to be afraid of. Although she'd never before experienced a hunger so intense and overpowering, never been propelled towards an unknown destination with such stark, unarguable urgency, she'd felt desire.

Five years ago it had been Greg...

Her mouth tightened against the sting of remembered grief. Yes, it had been instant attraction when she'd first met her golden, laughing Greg, an attraction that had deepened into love. But even with Greg she'd been able to control her desire until they'd made a commitment.

Nothing in her past had prepared her for the fierce need that now ached up from her bones, swamping her normal common sense in a tide of honeyed passion.

She'd taken one look at Alex and wanted him, everything that was sensible and civilised burnt away by the pale fire of his gaze and that indescribable aura that—reduced to the most primitive level—told each woman he met that he was a brilliant lover, a man who had the skills and prestige to care for her and her children.

Just like a peacock strutting his stuff, she thought, trying to demystify both Alex and her response to him. Male animals flaunted their colours and form before critical, choosy females; humans did it in much more subtle ways, but in the end it all came down to natural selection—the reason women liked intelligent men with social standing, the reason men went for beauty and youth in their wives.

Ianthe shook her head slightly and looked down at her hand, still winter pale on the arm of the chair. Weighed down by the exhaustion that gripped her each time she tried to deal with her water phobia, she endeavoured desperately to rally her scattered thoughts, only to find herself facing the unpalatable truth.

Even Greg hadn't awakened such deep and consuming needs in her. He'd been a darling, fun and intelligent and capable, and when he'd died she'd thought she'd die too, of grief. But she'd recovered. Oh, his death would always be a bruise on her soul, but she thought of him now only with love and regret.

Whereas this overwhelming, secret hunger was like nothing she'd experienced.

'I'm sorry about the interruption,' Alex said from behind her.

Ianthe jumped, hoping he didn't notice as she hastily straightened her spine. A glance revealed a grimness in his eyes and the cold, unreachable aura of withdrawal.

Chilled, she said swiftly, 'Don't be sorry. Actually, I should go home now.'

His brows drew together. 'I'm expecting another call and it might take a while. Would you like to lie down?'

What about Mark? He must have seen the query in her expression because he said, 'Mark's gone into Dargaville. If I'd realised you wanted to go back—'

'It's all right,' she said quickly. She'd violated the first commandment of all sensible women—make sure you have your own wheels—and she'd have to pay for it. 'I'll just sit out here and enjoy the view.'

'This spot gets too hot from now on,' he said, hooded, watchful gaze scrutinising her. 'Come on through—the sitting room's much cooler. Or there's a daybed in one of the bedrooms that you can use.'

By then her weariness had almost overcome her. Covering an abrupt yawn with her hand, she looked up and met his eyes, clear and shimmering and cold as the light just before dawn, and said reluctantly, 'I'm being a nuisance.'

'Nonsense,' he said, and held out his hand to help her out of the chair.

As deftly as she could, she avoided it, and walked a little distance from him to a bedroom decorated with the same spare luxury of the rest of the house. She looked at the daybed and yearned to lie on it and sleep.

'Shower if you want to,' Alex said. 'The bathroom's just through there.'

He nodded at a door in the wall and went out. Ianthe stood for a moment, her eyes blank as she clenched her fists by her sides. Then she drew a deep, deliberate breath and walked across the tiled floor to the bathroom. It was huge, with a shower bigger than the usual bath, and floor-length windows that looked out over the lake. Towels hung neatly; was he expecting a guest? 'None of your business,' she said curtly to her reflection.

After washing her feet she pulled back the light coverlet on the bed and lay down, heavy lids closing over her eyes almost immediately.

She woke to the sound of her name, and lifted slow lashes to see Alex standing by the daybed, his tanned face angular and honed into a predatory leanness, eyes glimmering beneath dark lashes. As she sat up the hard, intent recklessness disappeared, wiped clear by a self-control so determined she almost flinched.

'All right?' he asked.

Her voice lost in her dry throat, she nodded.

'I think I'd better get you home,' he said. 'People are waking up on the other side of the world, and it looks as though it's going to be a busy night for me.'

Well, no doubt billionaires had to see to their empires. She'd been right to link him to those barons of old; he was their equivalent, a modern conquistador carving out a realm for himself in the almost limitless territory of computers, software and the Internet.

She fought back a yawn. 'Do you stay up all night?'

'Not usually.' He smiled as she got to her feet, but although the potent masculine charm was as strong as ever his eyes remained masked. 'It's just that events on the other side of the world are moving fast, and need my personal attention. I'll see you in the sitting room when you're ready.'

Although sunset was hours away, the sky outside was tinged with the hot, melancholy drowsiness of a dying afternoon. Sleeping in the daytime always wrung Ianthe out, and today this was compounded by the knowledge that she'd been foolish to come here. As she washed her face and combed her hair and slipped her sandals back on she thought grimly that if she saw any more of Alex Considine she'd be wilfully heading into danger. One of the clearest indications of that was her heartache at the thought of never seeing him again!

It was time to call a halt, and this time she'd stick to her decision.

In the sitting room she said, 'If you're going to be busy, perhaps Mark could drive me home. That's if he's back.'

He said, 'He's back, but my mother always told me that if you took a girl out you had to take her home.'

'She has high principles, your mother.'

His mouth compressed and for a moment the chiselled features revealed a startling harshness. 'Very high.'

They drove home silently past the dim, fern-fresh glades where cicadas sang their shrill hymn to summer. On the other side of the road dairy cattle walked in a sedate file from the milking shed, swishing their tails against the flies and watching the car with mild interest.

'Take care,' Alex said when he left her at her door.

Ianthe turned and looked at him. 'You too,' she said, making the words a farewell.

He knew it; rejection flared like icy fire in his eyes and his face hardened. For seconds they stood motionless in the still air, the excited yelps and cries of bathing children fading into a hot, thick anticipation as they stared at each other.

His mouth twisted. With a swift, involuntary movement he caught her and bent his head and kissed her, his lips savage and passionate on hers, branding her. The fires of her own response took over and she obeyed their imperative orders and surrendered, offering her mouth, accepting his, taking what she could from that dangerous, tempting kiss.

At length he lifted his head, the clear eyes turbid now, his mouth a thin line, that air of predatory hunger so pronounced Ianthe shivered.

'I should apologise,' he said in a raw voice, 'but I'm not going to. I've been wanting to do that ever since I first saw you. You've got the mouth of a siren, a temptress, and I want you. But it's not going to happen.'

Although he wasn't asking a question, she shook her head. 'No,' she said quietly. Of course it wasn't going to happen. She had little to offer a man like Alex Considine. Instead of the impossibly glamorous, fascinating women he must mix with, she was just a small-time television personality and scientist with an ugly scar and a permanent limp.

He said harshly, 'You want me too.'

'Wanting doesn't seem to cover it, somehow,' she admitted, her voice a slow blend of irony and bitterness. 'Craving? Hunger? An obsession? Whatever it is I don't like it, and I'm not going to do anything about it because it terrifies me and I know there's no future for us, but if you want to satisfy your ego, then yes, I want you.'

He laughed humourlessly, astounding her by taking her

hand. With a gesture as courtly as it was ancient, he kissed the back of it, before turning it over and biting the mound at the base of her thumb with exactly calculated precision. When she gasped, torn by a knife-blade of sensation, he kissed the delicate blue veins at her wrist.

Eyes dilating, Ianthe snatched her hand back and pressed it against her breast.

Alex watched the rapid rise and fall of her breathing beneath the thin material of her shirt for a tense second before lifting his gaze to hold her captive with his dark, humourless smile. 'Do you believe in reincarnation, Ianthe?'

'No,' she said without even thinking.

'Neither do I, and yet—when I saw you that first time I wondered whether we'd met before, because your beautiful face, your husky siren's voice, your glorious hair were as familiar to me as my own.'

'You'd probably seen one of the documentaries,' she said gruffly, every cell in her body clamouring at the way his features were clamped in something like pain, his hard control for once failing him.

'No.' Black brows met above piercing, hooded eyes. In a rough, tight voice he said, 'I have decisions to make, decisions that won't wait, and you are not a woman for short, convenient liaisons.' For a second frustration rode him hard, edging his features with anger until he reined his emotions back and finished, 'I can't help hoping that in another life we meet again and finish what we've started at such an inopportune time here.'

Mesmerised, she was held defenceless by the blazing need in his eyes.

'I wish you happiness,' he said with an odd, set formality, and turned and walked away.

Ianthe forced herself to unlock the door, to walk in and close it behind her, to stand with her spine pressed against it until she heard the car purr away.

Why hadn't he tried to persuade her into an affair? He wouldn't have had to try very hard...

As soon as the thought coalesced, she rejected it. If he was a man like that she wouldn't be snared in this violent, wild attraction. One of the things that had drawn her was the integrity she'd sensed in him.

'And who do you think you're fooling? His *integrity* certainly attracted you,' she said out loud, the scornful words battering her confidence, 'but don't forget his face, and his body, and the power and magnetism of his personality. And his eyes...'

What decisions did he have to make? Or was he just letting her off lightly, because she wasn't the sort of woman for a man like him and he knew it even while he wanted her?

'Oh, why not just go ahead and *wallow* in self-pity?' she asked herself angrily.

Over the years she'd fought her lack of confidence and usually won. She knew where it came from; the day she'd discovered that her handsome, laughing father had left her and her mother, she'd become convinced that she hadn't been a good enough girl for him. Or for any man.

Logic and maturity told her that she was entirely wrong, and only rarely did that nasty sense of inferiority come sneaking back. Sometimes she wondered whether she'd agreed to do the documentaries just to show her father. Oh, not the man who did his dutiful best for her now, but the almost mythical father who'd abandoned her.

She spent too long in the shower, trying to wash her foolishness away, then walked along the beach, making herself nod a greeting to passersby, talk to small children, smile at harried mothers and fathers, at teenagers conducting their tentative, casual, yet elaborate wooings.

Once again she forced herself into the water; panic hit, but this time it was manageable. Oh, the images of teeth and blood and pain still laid siege to her emotions, yet a

bittersweet regret that came perilously close to grief almost
cancelled out terror.

Eventually she went back to the bach and brewed a pot
of coffee, drinking it on the back porch while the sun went
down.

Although she made herself read a book she'd been looking forward to for months, and then watched television until
her eyes were gritty, she didn't sleep. Prey to a consuming,
hurtful desire, she lay in her bed and planned out her future
in a world that didn't have Alex Considine in it.

She'd done it before; she could do it again. It just needed
will-power and self-control and perseverance, and she had
all of those qualities. She'd get there.

She had to.

Dawn broke onto a sky filmed with high clouds, sure sign
of a change in the weather. To keep her mind off the man
who'd expected to spend a busy night dealing with business
on the other side of the world, Ianthe switched on the radio
as she made toast and listened for the weather forecast.

When it finished she snapped it off, frowning. The Met
Service was being cagey, but if Cyclone Dara held its
present course and speed it would arrive at Northland the
next day as Cyclonic Storm Dara, and might give Northland
a battering. Campers were advised to listen to subsequent
forecasts.

Toast in hand, Ianthe went out and checked the sky
again. The lake's surface was ruffled by a wind from the
east, the filmy sky leaching colour from the waters.

There was no reason to worry; the bach had stood for
over fifty years. Although cyclonic storms dumped a lot of
rain and ripped off an occasional roof, usually the only
people who were troubled by them were those in tents and
caravans and boats, and farmers with low-lying land.

Of course there was the very occasional rogue, but she'd
be just as safe here as she would be anywhere.

Besides, she had no place to go. When she'd joined the

Sea Rover she'd given up her flat in the Bay of Islands and put her furniture in storage. Since the shark attack she'd spent much of her time in hospital, reluctantly moving to her father's house between operations.

She hadn't enjoyed that. Neither he nor his wife were unkind, or even unwelcoming, but Ianthe had been a burden. When Tricia's parents had offered the bach to recuperate in she'd accepted with delight.

Had Alex heard the storm was definitely on the way? Perhaps she should ring the house and tell him.

Except that she didn't have his number. Of course she could always ask at the store—they'd almost certainly know—but she wouldn't, because what she was doing was trying to find a good reason for contacting him again.

Even though he'd told her that he always listened to the weather forecast.

Anyway, she had things to do, and the first one was checking the garage. Arrayed around its walls and at the rear were various odds and ends that Tricia's father had thought might come in handy one day. Amongst the crayfish pots and the knotted fishing lines, the cane chair that no one had ever taken to be mended and the plastic-wrapped inflatable mattresses, Ianthe found an old Primus stove with a dusty bottle of kerosene, and even some methylated spirits to get it going.

Just to make sure she remembered how to do it, she took it into the kitchen, cleaned it, then lit it, looking with satisfaction as the blue flames formed a ring around the burner. It was good to know she hadn't lost her touch. If the power went off she'd be able to cook and make tea.

Switching the Primus off, she drove down to the store and bought enough groceries to last her a couple of days.

'Not leaving?' the woman behind the counter asked with a quick smile.

'No. I suppose the forecast will drive most people home.'

The woman looked harried, as well she might. She probably expected to earn half her annual income from the summer holiday season. 'Not yet,' she said. 'The cyclone won't cause us any problems—no creeks run into the lakes so they don't flood, and we're pretty sheltered—but if it's going to rain for three days you can't blame people for deciding they might as well be at home. Still, with any luck it'll fizzle out and die somewhere north of Cape Reinga. We'll probably get a bit of rain like we did in the ones before Christmas, that's all.'

'The farmers will be happy,' Ianthe said, accepting her purchases.

The woman's worried frown lifted and she gave a conspiratorial grin. 'Want to bet? When have you ever known a farmer to be happy? Still, last year we really suffered with a drought. A good year for farmers puts money into the district.'

And no doubt a good year for the camping ground and store did the same.

Back at the bach, Ianthe unpacked the groceries, then decided that she'd wash the clothes. After hanging sheets and towels and clothes out, she swept the bach, remade the bed and dusted the furniture.

By then it was almost lunchtime and the weather was clearly deteriorating. A wind sprang up from the east, still hot and carrying humidity with it, and teased the surface of the lake into waves. While Ianthe made a sandwich she listened to the forecast, frowning when she heard that the cyclone had sped up. If it kept to the same path—by no means a certainty—it would strike Northland some time the following morning.

After lunch she gathered all the chairs from the porch and transferred them to the garage, and then there was nothing more to do—no garden to cosset, no plants to tie up. Tricia's parents very sensibly paid one of the local high school boys to keep the lawn mown, and apart from the big macrocarpa cypress at the front, the only other plants on the property were a pear tree so ancient it no longer bore fruit, and a lemon tree noted more for the size and ferocity of its thorns than for its lemons.

For a moment she stood there, staring at the sky, sightlessly fixing on clouds that had begun to wear the tattered, driven aspect of an approaching storm, then retired to the verandah, watching the few swimmers, the radio beside her so she could listen to the forecasts, which she did with ever-increasing concern.

Cyclone Dara was not the usual storm, losing intensity as it came south into cooler waters. The Met Service forecasts were guarded, but as the afternoon wore on they assumed a more sombre tone, warning everyone to get out of its path if they could, or to take precautions for what promised to be an extremely nasty experience.

And people were listening. As she watched caravans and campervans began to pull out of the camp.

At least, Ianthe thought, trying to look on the bright side as she gathered in clean clothes from the line, she didn't have to worry about large areas of glass. The bach's small-paned windows were much more likely to endure a cyclonic wind than sheets of plate glass. And the macrocarpa tree would shelter it from the direct force of an easterly wind.

She was folding the clothes when the next-door neighbour, a large man whose red hair was a vivid and rather shocking contrast to his ruddy skin, arrived with an Auckland telephone number and a request. 'If anything goes wrong, will you let us know?'

'Of course I will. Are you leaving now?'

'Yes,' he said. 'The wife wants to be at home if this thing hits us. I reckon she feels a bit exposed in the bach, and the weather people say it's going to come ashore round about here.'

'These baches have coped with everything the weather's thrown at them since they were built,' Ianthe said comfortingly, 'so I wouldn't worry. Drive carefully.'

'Oh, don't you worry about that. Take care.' He gave her a quick smile and turned to go, then stopped and walked back. 'By the way, keep an eye on that macrocarpa,' he said, knitting his brows. 'A couple of years ago a big branch came down in a winter storm. I told Vince then he should cut the tree down, but he said it was sound at the heart and would outlive us all.'

Ianthe followed his gaze. The tree was massive, its outstretched branches covering most of the front lawn.

'It doesn't overshadow the bach,' she pointed out.

He shook his head. 'If the wind gets strong enough to tear a branch off, it'll be strong enough to smash it into the bach. If the wind comes from the west, don't hesitate—go to our place. Here.' He fished in his pocket and held out a key on a key-ring from which bobbed a troll with green hair. 'This is to the back door.'

'I can't take your key—'

'We've got another one. You take it now—you just might need it. I'll feel happier if you do.'

Because he looked so anxious she accepted it. Still frowning, he nodded, repeated his injunction to take care, and only then left, turning to wave from the roadside where his car, towing a boat on its trailer, waited.

After seeing them off Ianthe walked around the tree, eyeing the scar. It was on the opposite side of the tree from the bach, and she couldn't see any tell-tale sign of decay in the trunk, but her stomach clenched slightly as she walked around to the verandah. Since the last forecast the traffic had built up; now a stream of campervans, cyclists, cars towing boats, cars with roof racks piled high and cars towing caravans was leaving the camping ground.

She had the disconcerting feeling that by the time the visitors had all gone she'd be the sole person left to batten down what hatches needed to be battened. Which was ridiculous, because the locals would be toughing it out too.

In the late afternoon the rain came, spitting at first, and then in gusts driven before the rapidly rising wind. And twenty minutes after that there was a knock on the door.

She opened it to find Mark standing there. Disappoint-

ment arced through her like an electric shock. 'Hello,' she
said uncertainly.

'Hi.' He looked around what he could see of the bach.
'Mr Considine sent me to find out if you were all right.'

'I'm fine, thank you.' So Alex hadn't left with all the
others. She stepped back and gestured. 'Everything's under
control.'

Mark glowered around. 'This thing doesn't look as
though it would stand up to a storm, let alone a hurricane.'

'You're a New Zealander—you know we don't have hur-
ricanes,' Ianthe said. 'And cyclones lose their strength as
the waters get colder.'

Mark said, 'They can do a hell of a lot of damage, just
the same.'

'We're sheltered by the hills,' Ianthe said. 'Tell Mr
Considine not to worry; he'll be perfectly safe.'

It was a malicious little jab, but Mark didn't seem to
notice. 'He's not worried about himself,' he said. 'That
house is built to stand the end of the world.'

Ianthe repeated what she'd already said several times that
day. 'This bach is over fifty years old; it'll take more than
a cyclone to shift it.'

He turned to look at the dark bulk of the macrocarpa, its
stiff branches beginning to toss. 'How old's that?'

She shrugged. 'No idea, but it's been here a long time
too, and survived other cyclones. Thank Mr Considine for
thinking of me, but tell him not to worry—I'll be fine.'

Massive shoulders lifted slightly. 'OK,' he said, and
walked back to the Range Rover.

Ianthe closed the door. Alex had done what any decent
man would have done, and done it in the only sensible way.

She kept trying to convince herself of that as the wind
began to whine around the eaves and the waters of the lake
roiled beneath the scudding, driving rain. Not only did she
not want to see him again, she couldn't afford to. They'd
said goodbye; anything else would be an anti-climax.

But it hurt that he hadn't come himself.

Ianthe frowned at the grey waters of the lake, whipped into waves by the increasing wind. Rain slashed down in slanted sheets—not yet steady enough to be called a downpour, but picking up intensity as time dragged by.

Another knock on the door—sharp, peremptory—coincided with the flickering and eventual death of the lightbulb in the centre light.

'Damn!' she muttered. She had a gas lantern, and candles and matches, but losing the power at this early stage was a bad sign.

She opened the door and there was Alex, rain sleeking his black hair, those pale eyes narrowed and dangerous.

'You'd better pack some clothes,' he said abruptly, before she had time to speak, 'because I agree with Mark—that tree is too big and too damned close. All it needs is one weak branch and you could be crushed. So get whatever you need for a couple of days. You can stay with me.'

'I can't,' she said crisply.

'Why not?' He looked tough and determined and uncompromising.

'I promised I'd keep an eye on the bach next door. If I'm worried about the tree I can go there—I've got a key.'

His brows drew together. 'Don't be an idiot,' he said caustically. 'When branches start hurtling around it won't be safe for you to go outside.'

Ianthe said stubbornly, 'I told Mr Robertson—'

'I'll get you back the minute the storm finishes,' he said, his mouth hardening.

She drew in a deep breath, calling on all her reserves of strength to face down his compelling, forceful urgency. 'Alex—'

'I hope,' he said with studied brutality, 'you don't feel that I'm likely to leap on you and demand that you pay me for my hospitality?'

It wasn't so much the words, although they were crude enough, but the tone of his voice that made every hair on the back of her neck stand upright. He sounded disgusted, and when her gaze flew up to meet his she could have cried out at the frigid distaste she saw in their cold depths.

He'd seen into her secret, unspoken—unthought—hopes, and he didn't need to tell her what he thought of them.

'No!' she returned explosively. 'Of course I don't—'

A wild gust shook the windows of the bach, and a heavy, loud crack jerked them both around as a small upper branch tore off the macrocarpa and lurched, twigs flailing, towards the bach. Ianthe drew in a sudden, shocked breath when it thudded onto the grass some twenty feet away.

Harshly, Alex said, 'Right, that's it. Get some clothes or I'll get them for you. You're coming with me.'

CHAPTER FIVE

DRY-MOUTHED, Ianthe stared while the heavy, layered branches of the tree thrashed against the leaden sky, then settled back as the gust roared on past.

'Once one's gone others are likely to,' Alex said inflexibly.

'I know.' She ironed out a catch in her voice. 'Can we strengthen the windows?'

'We haven't got time,' he said. 'That's only the forerunner—the wind will settle into a proper gale, and by then we need to be gone. Ianthe, get a move on!'

Faced by his driving, relentless will, she surrendered. In her bedroom she scooped clothes and necessities into a bag, collected shoes and the book she was reading.

When she got back into the sitting room he closed the door of the fridge and picked up the plastic bags into which he'd packed its contents. 'All ready?' he asked, and gave her an abrupt, blazing smile that sent her heart soaring.

'Yes,' she said simply. 'Shall I bring the Primus? I've got a lantern too.'

'No, I've got gas appliances.'

Outside it was eerily still. He was driving the Range Rover, and as he started the engine Ianthe said, 'Being pushed into a ditch by a truck didn't do much damage to this.'

'It needed a new mudguard, that's all.'

Nevertheless it was remarkable that it had been fixed so rapidly. But then, she thought, staring ahead as they drove past the motor camp, if you were a software billionaire you probably got things done overnight, even during the

Christmas holidays in New Zealand. She cast a glance at his angular profile.

He had, she thought, trying to ease the constriction in her chest, the most unrevealing face she'd ever known. It was as though his stunning good looks were a mask that hid the inner man with complete efficiency. Was he angry that his overblown sense of responsibility had forced him to collect her?

Halfway there, Ianthe broke into the silence. 'That one blast of wind might be it, you know.'

'A one-gust cyclone?' He sounded amused. 'It doesn't seem likely.'

Again she glanced sideways, noting the crease in his cheek when he smiled. It didn't soften the angles and planes that gave him his severe male beauty, or the determined line of jaw and chin, but it made her bones melt.

Turning her head hastily, she said the first thing that came into her brain. 'The creeks aren't up yet.'

'It hasn't been raining long enough.'

She nodded, and stuck with the nice safe topic. 'One thing, because no creeks run into the lakes they won't get polluted with run-off.'

'That would explain the clarity of their water.'

He was humouring her in this stupid conversation. Irritated, she relapsed into silence.

Once at the house, Ianthe was struck by the emptiness. Looking around, she asked, 'Where's Mark?'

'I sent him home.' When Ianthe's brows rose he explained calmly, 'His sister lives by herself at the beach and he was worried about her.'

Ianthe felt mean; when Mark had said something about the force of the cyclone she hadn't thought of him being personally concerned. 'It's a bit difficult to imagine Mark with a family,' she said foolishly.

He shrugged. 'Everyone has family, even if they've managed to lose them.'

Some undertone to the words—unsparing, yet more than

a little ironic—drew her gaze to his face. The pitiless clarity of his eyes revealed nothing but an icy blueness. How could eyes so transparent be so opaque?

'I lost mine,' she volunteered.

'What happened?'

Driven by another squall, rain shrouded the windows, darkening the room to a sombre twilight. Ianthe shivered. 'My father left when I was seven. He found another wife, had another family, and after that he wasn't interested in me.'

'He abandoned you?'

The formidable note of condemnation in his voice elicited a swift answer. 'He made sure my mother had enough money, and he paid for me to go to a very good school and on to university. I had anything I wanted.'

'Anything but a father,' he said quietly.

Shrugging, she returned, 'It happens all the time.'

'And your mother?'

Ianthe walked across to gaze outside. The clouds had robbed the lake of colour, but even so she could see the stark rim where the bottom sank away from the shore.

'When I went away to university,' she said flatly, 'she committed suicide. In her letter she said she no longer had anything left to live for now that I'd left her. We'd quarrelled for a whole year because I wanted to leave home.'

She hadn't realised that she'd hugged herself, keeping the cold at bay, until his arms enfolded her. At their strength and heat, and the subtle, intoxicating scent of his body, excitement began to drum a compelling beat through her veins.

'I'd wanted to get away,' Ianthe said bleakly, holding herself stiffly against his too-seductive warmth, the support he offered. 'She clung—she was afraid of losing me, and I was careless and thoughtless. I didn't realise how much she needed me, how much she loved me.'

'It's an odd sort of love that denies freedom.' He spoke

in an inflexible, unsparing tone, but the arms around her were wonderfully comforting.

'I should have tried to understand. Looking back, I can see that she had to use most of her emotional energy just to hold herself together. My father said once that he couldn't live with her because she was so highly strung and jealous. He exaggerated, but she was always tired and intense and stressed.'

'And of course you wonder whether she'd have been all right if you'd stayed.'

His voice reverberated through her. Against his chest she nodded, swallowing back the words that ached in her throat.

'She used emotional blackmail,' he said levelly, 'and when that didn't work she made sure you'd suffer for it. If she was so fragile that your decision to go to university drove her to commit suicide, you'd have probably spent all your life doing what she wanted, submerging your existence in hers so that she didn't fly into pieces.'

Averting her face, Ianthe said bleakly, 'I could have got her help.'

'How old were you?'

'Seventeen,' she admitted.

'Too young to have that responsibility. Besides, she could have got help for herself if she'd wanted to.'

Chilled by his hard logic, she stepped away. Hot pulses of sensation still throbbed through her, but at least she had control over her voice.

Without looking at him she said, 'I'll never know. And although I grieve for her despair, I don't blame myself.' Her mouth twisted. 'My father paid for a very good therapist who said the same as you. It just doesn't seem fair that it had to be that—her life or mine.'

'I understand.' He spoke reflectively, that odd foreign intonation suddenly there. 'But by punishing you for leaving her she made her choice. It wasn't your choice.'

'I don't know,' Ianthe said quietly. 'I just don't know.'

She stared through the rain and changed the subject. 'If all we get is rain we're going to be lucky.'

'Let's hope the wind stays out to sea,' he said.

She eyed the strip of sand, eerily white in the grey light. 'How often do you get here?'

'At least once a year.' Some hidden emotion shaded the deep texture of his voice. 'More often if I can manage it, but most years I can't.'

'Your architect's a miracle-worker.'

'He's a New Zealander,' he said. 'A chap called Philip Angove who lives in a superb house on the Kaipara Harbour. He runs a large station down there, but in his heart he's an architect—one of the best New Zealand's got. He designs houses for selected people, and I consider myself very fortunate to have persuaded him to do this one for me.'

Ianthe stared at him. 'I've met him,' she said. 'In fact, he and his wife came to dinner at my father's.'

Much to her stepmother's delight! The Angoves were old money, although Philip Angove's wife Antonia had come out of nowhere to marry him. Neither wore their heart on their sleeves, but they were a devoted couple. Interesting too; Ianthe had enjoyed their company very much.

'He's certainly a genius,' she said. 'Too many people try to fit suburbia into the wilderness.'

'Marigolds,' he said, and laughed softly.

Her neighbours at the lake had planted several rows of marigolds in front of their bach. The gaudy, shaggy heads looked supremely out of place in the quiet harmony of land and sky and water.

She grinned. 'Exactly.'

They stood in silence watching the steady, prodigal rain as it poured onto the dimpled surface of the lake in its endless cycle of renewal and change.

Tension—thin and dangerous as a blade—sliced through Ianthe's composure with its edged ambivalence, part threat, part excitement, mixed with an eager, urgent anticipation.

This was how she'd felt the first time she'd dived through the wall of blue all those years ago; years later, she'd experienced the same awe swimming with dolphins, and then seeing for the first time the life around the coral reefs—and that had also been her scared, stunned response to sleek, primeval sharks when she'd seen them from the comparative safety of the shark cage.

But she wasn't secure behind mesh and bars now.

She'd never felt such untamed, consuming expectancy before—not even with the man she'd lost to death. She'd loved Greg with her whole heart, and had mourned him for years, until eventually she remembered him with no more than gratitude and nostalgia. He'd laughed a lot, had Greg, and kissed her fears and worries away, and radiated a warmth she couldn't resist.

Whereas Alex walked on the cold side, his forceful vitality reined by his will into an uncompromising strength that intimidated her. When he'd believed they would never meet again he'd kissed her with fire and passion and a fierce urgency that had scorched through the barriers, but this last embrace had been impersonal. He'd intended to comfort, and was determined not to let it go beyond that.

'Would you like something to drink?' Alex asked. 'It looks like a long night ahead.'

She said sedately, 'I would, thank you.'

His movements were sure and deft, and he made excellent coffee. It surprised her that he should be competent in the kitchen. Greg had been an only son with two doting older sisters; he'd been indulged from birth, and she'd indulged him too. For the first time she wondered whether she'd have continued spoiling him, or whether some day she'd have been irritated by his calm assumption that someone would always minister to his needs.

Times change, she thought impatiently, because her thoughts seemed disloyal. Times change, and I've changed too. I'm twenty-six, not twenty-one. You can't go back.

Opening the pantry doors, Alex removed a biscuit tin, prised off the lid and held out the tin.

'These look home-made,' she said, taking one. 'Oh, afghans—my favourite biscuit in all the world.'

'Mark baked them,' Alex said, and laughed quietly at her astonishment.

She bit into the sweet, crunchy texture, and when she'd swallowed said, 'Do you think he might teach me how to make them? They're delicious.'

'You could always ask. Apparently he also makes sponge cakes, but they're not a favourite of mine so he's been concentrating on afghans.'

Did Mark do all the cooking, or was Alex capable of producing a meal? Ianthe reined the question back. She wanted to know too much about him, and he wasn't going to tell her anything.

Why on earth had she blurted out her family story? Colour, clammy and embarrassing, swept across her skin with sticky speed.

Back in the sitting room, she said in her most composed voice, 'Even in this weather, your rooms look sunny and summery. You must have had a very good decorator.'

'Very good,' he said.

All right, she thought mutinously, I don't care if you clam up again.

She drank some coffee and refused another biscuit, settling back into her chair, ignoring the lengthening silence. He could come up with a topic of conversation.

Alex said tonelessly, 'My father was killed when I was ten.'

Fragments of shocked thought jostled around Ianthe's brain. She blinked. 'That must have been terrible,' she said uncertainly.

'I idolised him and so did my mother. We were poor, but with my father life was a rich feast.'

He certainly didn't behave as if he'd grown up in poverty—such cool, uncompromising confidence was usually the prerogative of those born to wealth and authority.

Aloud she said, 'That's quite a legacy.'

'Yes.' His face hardened, but the momentary grimness disappeared as quickly as it came and his classical features were impassive when he went on, 'My father's death shattered my mother, yet although she had nothing she managed to make a new life for us.'

'Is she still alive?'

Heavy lids lifted a second, then fell. 'Very much so.'

It was foolish to see his natural reserve as rejection. He was merely protecting his privacy. No doubt he'd experienced the toadying and favour-seeking that too much money and power could cause. After all, he didn't know that she wouldn't head off to one of the tabloids and reveal all, that the few times they'd met and touched wouldn't be splashed over newspapers for the prurient to read.

Yet it hurt. He should realise she wasn't like that—she knew the thought was unreasonable even as it formed in her brain.

After a swift glance at his watch he said, 'Do you mind if I put the television on?'

'No, of course I don't.'

The set—a thin screen with little apparent space for working parts—lurked behind the doors of a very modern cabinet. Alex switched it on to Teletext and sat back. In silence they read the reports of the cyclone's progress, all ominous, which were followed on the warning band with a Northland-wide forecast indicating that the cyclone was expected to hit the west coast.

Alex turned the set off and said, 'That sounds definite enough. Even if it takes a last-minute detour we're going to get enough wind and rain to make life uncomfortable.'

'It certainly looks like it.' She startled herself by giving a sudden smile. 'You were pretty high-handed, but I'm glad I'm here. I wouldn't have liked being alone.'

'I'm surprised your father didn't insist on you returning

to Auckland,' he said, not bothering to hide the note of condemnation in the words.

Ianthe sat up a little straighter. 'My father hasn't had any control over my actions for a long time,' she said. 'Could you show me where I'm to sleep, please? I'll unpack, and then perhaps I could help you with dinner?'

'I'd be grateful for any help I can get,' he said, getting to his feet with the lithe economy of movement that sent tiny, erotic shudders along her nerves. 'I'm a reasonable plain cook, but that's as far as it goes.'

As he picked up her overnight bag and showed her to the room she'd slept in before, she asked, 'Why do we have electricity when the power was off at the other lakes?'

'Our supply comes in from the north,' he said. 'Now, do you have everything you want?'

'Yes, thank you.'

When she emerged again they watched the news, sitting in silence as the newsreader told everyone that on-the-spot teams would be reporting in frequently. The weatherman showed the cyclone—an alarming spiral of cloud—and again warned everyone in Northland to move stock to higher ground, to check doors and windows, to stay inside.

It was followed by a lighter item about royalty. Ianthe picked up a magazine and began scanning its pages idly.

Alex asked, 'Is it boring you? Shall I turn it off?'

'Oh—no, not if you want to watch.'

'I'd like to see the foreign news.'

'Yes, of course.'

'You're not a royalist, I gather.' His voice was detached.

'I feel so sorry for them—what sort of a life do they have?'

His brows rose. 'The same sort as rock stars and actors,' he pointed out objectively. 'You chose to front a television series knowing, I presume, that you'd be an object of interest to the media.'

'It didn't occur to me, but even so I *chose* to do it, like rock singers and Hollywood stars. And it is possible to keep their lives private if they want to, whereas royals are born into publicity—however much they might hate it, they have no choice.'

'Perhaps being born into it makes it easier,' he suggested mildly.

She shrugged. 'Friends of my mother's used to buy battery hens when they were too old to be profitable any more. They'd been carefully bred so that they didn't scratch, and didn't need to do all the things that make normal hens so happy. But when they were put out into the chook run they soon learned to scratch, and to fly, and to take dust baths. I admire modern royalty enormously for the job they do, but to me it seems like being enslaved.'

'Strong words,' he said, his eyes cool and shadowed.

More temperately, she answered, 'My father paid for my education at an exclusive school where one of the boarders was a girl from a very important family in an Asian country. In her last year she fell in love with a friend of her brother's who was at university, and they planned to elope. She knew she'd never be allowed to marry the man she loved—he wasn't important enough.'

He said nothing when she paused, and she went on, 'Her brother found out and alerted his father, and he took her home before she could actually run away. Within six weeks he'd married her off to another man—much older, but very suitable, according to his standards. I met her two or three years afterwards. She'd died inside. Oh, she was physically alive—she smiled and talked, and behaved like a human being—but there was nothing behind her eyes. I've never seen anyone sunk into such profound and appalling misery.'

'And you blame her parents for that?'

'In her society,' she said, embarrassed now by her anger, 'it's not just the parents, it's the whole family. I don't blame *them*—I blame a system that makes an important marriage more valuable than someone's happiness.'

'What you're talking about is the clash between a strongly family-oriented culture and the cult of individualism,' he observed, his neutral tone a contrast to her heat. 'Both have good points, both bad.'

Ianthe said, 'A hundred years ago it might have been necessary for her to sink her own needs and marry a man to uphold her family's social standing, but not nowadays.'

'In all situations there are those who win and those who lose,' he said. 'In a way your friend was like your mother—she could have chosen to live.'

'Perhaps so, but it's hard to do that when you are shown exactly what your value is as a living human being—nothing, merely a pawn to be used by your parents for their greatest advantage,' Ianthe retorted caustically.

The rapidly moving images on the screen altered. Grateful for the change, she leaned forward a little to gaze at the streets of the small city somewhere in the Balkans. A violent gust of wind struck the house; it died away almost immediately, but the rain intensified, drowning out the journalist's commentary.

Alex touched the control and the voice blared forth. 'There have been at least three deaths so far,' the reporter said, 'and it's believed that those who were dragged into the barracks are being denied medical care. Because many of the soldiers seemed unwilling to fire on their compatriots, the death rate could have been much higher. However, it's unlikely the ruling junta will surrender to popular opinion and go quietly, and as there's no sign of the lost prince further bloodshed is expected.'

The television clicked off, filling the room with the steady sound of the rain.

'I feel so sorry for the Illyrians,' Ianthe said, trying to diffuse some latent tension that had suddenly sprung to life. 'They've had such a wretched time—betrayed and betrayed again—and now it looks as though it's going to happen once more. Why must people cling to power?'

'God knows.' Alex's voice was sombre.

She said angrily, 'It's not as though it's much to cling to, for heaven's sake! A tiny country on the Adriatic, some minuscule leftover of the Byzantine Empire—why can't that wretched junta fly to a tax haven with the money they've stolen from the peasants and give them what they want?'

'Do you know what they want?' he asked, cool irony hardening his voice.

'Democracy, I suppose.'

His smile was empty of humour. 'Far from it. They want the return of their prince.'

'Their prince? Oh, you mean the lost prince? But that's just a legend.'

Leaning back into the big chair, he looked straight ahead, eyes half-closed, his autocratic profile a stark silhouette against the pale wall. 'They don't seem to think so.'

'Isn't he dead?'

'Almost certainly, but when you've been ruled for a thousand years by a prince I suppose it's hard to give up the habit.' His voice was level, without emotion.

Ianthe clamped down hard enough on her curiosity to achieve a neutral tone when she said, 'You seem to know a lot about such an insignificant place.'

'I have an interest there.'

For a moment she thought he was going to leave it like that, but he said off-handedly, 'My family had an Illyrian side. They're all dead now.'

No doubt there had been much intermarriage across the border between Illyria and Italy. A glance at his shuttered expression revealed that he wasn't going to say any more about his dead relatives.

Choosing her words carefully Ianthe asked, 'How did the princes kept their little realm intact through those centuries?'

'The country's basically a range of mountains with a big central valley and a tiny outlet to the coast. They have no minerals and the people were legendary for their ferocity.'

'So it wasn't worth fighting for.'

A smile creased his cheek. He turned his head and said blandly, 'You got it.'

'OK, for a thousand years they were left alone with their princes. How did they manage to lose the last one?'

'He disappeared when the communists took over.'

'Oh.' She sighed. 'I suppose they disposed of him, poor man.'

The broad shoulders lifted in a shrug. 'Nobody knows.'

Intrigued, Ianthe asked, 'Did he have a family?'

'He was married,' Alex said. 'Many Illyrians insist that he and his wife escaped. When communism crashed they had what were supposed to be democratic elections, but the politicians they elected were cut from the same cloth as their old leaders, and the people have had enough. Apparently they think that if they demonstrate for long enough their lost prince will come back and rescue them.'

'It sounds incredibly romantic and Ruritanian, but if he did escape and is still somewhere out there,' Ianthe said briskly, 'he's probably saying thanks, but no thanks, and getting on with his nice, normal life.'

His mouth curved. 'Is that what you'd do?'

'Oh, it is indeed,' she said fervently.

'Even though these people depend on him to save them?'

She stared into the leaping flames of the fire. 'I don't see how anyone who has got used to the joys of being ordinary could go back to that sort of life,' she said quietly.

'Even if it's his responsibility to go back?'

'You have an over-developed sense of responsibility,' she said. 'I feel really sorry for them, but a prince isn't going to save them, poor things.'

Evidently bored with the subject of the lost prince of Illyria, he changed the subject, and as the room slowly darkened they talked and talked and talked.

Alex was frighteningly clever, but of course he'd have to be. People didn't get to be software magnates without intelligence and an entrepreneurial flair amounting to genius. He was also a visionary, and that too went with the territory. He had an interest in, and opinions on, subjects that ranged from the possibility of inter-stellar travel to the worldwide death of frogs.

'Not,' she said, as the hollow booming of multitudes of them echoed through the room, 'that anyone's told the frogs in New Zealand they're supposed to be dying, thank heavens.'

'Do they keep you awake?'

'I'm used to them. In fact, I rather like the noise. I've been coming to the lakes for holidays all my life, and the sound means summer and holidays and fun to me.'

He got to his feet. When they'd come in he'd switched on a lamp, and he seemed to loom in the shadowy room, solid and lithe and very, very real. Another lamp suddenly bloomed, the swift glow outlining his features with an edge of gold as he straightened up.

He looked, Ianthe thought as her mouth dried, a very civilised man. His clothes were casual but they'd been made for him; from the neck down he could have stepped from the pages of one of the top men's magazines. Those hawkish features, however, gave him away; pirate features, she thought—the sheer handsomeness of his face utterly overawed by the dynamic strength imprinted there.

Except that 'imprinted' was the wrong word, because the strength was inherent, arising from the steely force of his character.

She knew so little about him, nothing much more than that he'd grown up in Australia before rising like a sky-rocket through the business world, not setting a foot wrong as he'd carved out his territory.

'Time to make some dinner,' he said. 'Is that offer of help still open?'

The meal was superb, a green pea soup accompanied by tasty little blue cheese toasts, followed by salmon fillet crumbed with couscous. Ianthe showed Alex how to make a lemon and dill mixture with sour cream to serve with the fish, and he found the lettuce and cress to make a green salad, with tomatoes an added bonus.

'Pudding?' he asked when the last golden crunch of salmon and couscous had been swallowed. 'There's fruit.'

'Heavens, no, thank you,' she said, and sighed. 'That was sublime, and you're a liar.'

He smiled. 'Why?'

'I wouldn't call that good plain cooking,' she said, a little unsteadily because his smile had pierced her with delight. 'It was wonderful—ambrosia—and this is the nectar.' She gave him a lazy grin that could probably be blamed on the half-empty glass of Reisling in her hand. 'Could I have the recipe for the salmon, please?'

He laughed quietly. 'Of course. I'm glad you enjoyed it—it's one of my mother's favourites.'

'I'm not a good cook,' she admitted, lulled by the fire and the food and the relaxed ambience. 'I've never really bothered to learn how to do it properly, but I can see I'll have to give it a go.'

They had talked of all sorts of things during the meal; nothing too personal, although he'd said he enjoyed reading legal thrillers and good travel writing, and liked opera.

She'd teased him about such an elitist taste, and he'd laughed and said, 'Opera is all about passions lived at full power, with glorious music and lives laid on the line. It's a blood sport—especially in Italy, where even the most adored tenor or soprano can get hissed off the stage if they don't come up to expectations.'

That was almost enough to persuade Ianthe to go to the next opera that came her way. She confessed her attachment to moody French films in black and white, starring sultry men and wicked, heartless women, and was surprised to find that he'd seen quite a few and enjoyed them too.

He was easy to talk to, she thought, as they washed the dishes. And yet—and yet, she sensed a barrier in him.

He looked up suddenly and smiled, and something clamped around her despairing heart. How fortunate that I haven't known him long enough to fall in love with him, she thought as she forced a weak smile in return.

The lights flickered and surrendered to the night.

'Damn,' Alex said in the darkness, his voice cool and restrained. 'Never mind, I'll get a torch and light the gas lamps. We've got gas for cooking too, so we won't starve. Would you like a cup of coffee?'

Her eyes strained through the firelit room, making out the darker shadow that was him. Keeping her voice level, she said, 'Yes, thank you.'

In the warm, mellow glow of a gas lamp they made coffee and drank it while outside the constant din of the rain on the roof protected them from the rest of the world.

And through the casual conversation tension stretched tighter and tighter in Ianthe. When I've finished the coffee, she decided, I'll make some excuse and go to bed.

She'd just set her empty cup down on its saucer when someone hammered on the back door. Starting, she glanced around. 'Why on earth is anyone out on a night like this?'

'I'll go and find out,' Alex said.

She got to her feet, but stayed where she was, watching the light of the lamp progress down the short corridor that led to the back door. A sharp increase in the sound of rain meant the door was open; she heard a muffled exclamation, and then the light came back as Alex returned with a thin woman in her late forties or early fifties. Her hair and skin glistened with moisture, and she looked around, clearly searching for someone else.

Alex commanded, 'Get a cup of coffee for Mrs—'

'Shandon,' the woman supplied, her teeth chattering, 'but we haven't got time. Isn't Mark here?'

'No.'

The woman dragged in a shuddering breath. 'I thought he'd be here,' she said, and fell silent, staring at Alex with a bewildered expression as though whatever had driven her to his door had suddenly evaporated and she was awakening from a dream.

'Why do you want Mark?' Alex asked gently, urging her onto a chair as Ianthe poured out coffee, added milk and sugar, and wrapped the woman's cold hands around the mug.

'My husband went out to move some stock,' the woman said, eyeing the mug with the same bewilderment with which she might view an alien artefact. Although great shivers shook her slender frame she was clearly trying to marshal her thoughts. 'He moved them all onto higher ground yesterday, but he came down to Dargaville today. I'm a charge nurse at the hospital, and our grandson's in there with meningitis—well, he's getting better, but it's his birthday today... He's only three...'

Her voice tailed away and Alex said quietly, 'So your husband moved the stock.'

'Yes.' Focusing on his face, she paused, then said more calmly, 'I spent some time with Joey—my grandson—so I didn't get back until after six, but Rob had left a note on the table. The heifers had broken through the fence into the Spit paddock, down by the creek, so he went to shift them out of there and away from any flooding.'

Ianthe guided the mug to her lips. Obediently Mrs Shandon drank.

Waiting until she stopped, Alex asked, 'Did he put the time on his note?'

'Oh, yes.' She looked at her watch. 'Three hours ago,' she said, pushing the mug away. 'I went as far as I could, but the creek's right up and the bridge is gone. I couldn't see him or any of the stock. We know Mark well—he and Rob help each other quite often—so I came here.' She stopped abruptly and bit her lip.

Ianthe urged her to drink again as Alex asked, 'Have you contacted anyone else?'

'The phone line's down. Anyway, no one can get through because there's a slip just past your gate. The bank's collapsed in the cutting—as I turned into your gateway I could see the rocks and mud all over the road.'

Alex nodded. 'Drink up that coffee while I see if I can raise anyone on the cellphone.'

When he came back in Mrs Shandon put down her almost empty mug. 'Can anyone come?'

'No,' he said. 'How did you get here?'

'In the car.'

'We'll go back in the Range Rover,' he said. 'We can't expect any help—even if they could clear the slip. The Civil Defence operator said that emergency services are already overloaded with a pile-up on the road south of Dargaville. As well, it's going to be high tide when they expect the cyclone to hit, so they're evacuating people. And there's no way anyone will get a chopper off the ground in this weather.'

CHAPTER SIX

TEN minutes later they were driving along a road running with water. The headlights cut a swathe through the darkness—a swathe filled with crystal needles of rain, solid, heavy, relentless. The sombre mass of pines crowded against one side, contrasting with the gleaming green of the paddocks on the other.

'Did your husband go on the tractor?' Alex asked.

Mrs Shandon, although still very tense, had been won over by his calm competence. 'No,' she said, 'he took the quad.'

A four-wheeled farm bike.

Alex asked, 'Have you got a tractor?'

'Yes.'

'Then we'll use that.'

The woman asked, 'Can you drive one? I'm afraid I can't.' After a moment's pause she explained defensively, 'We've had sharemilkers until this last year, so I haven't bothered to keep up with each new tractor—and this one is huge.' Her voice hardened. 'Believe me, from now on I'm going to learn how to drive or ride every piece of equipment we've got.'

Alex said, 'I spent my high school holidays working a bulldozer. I'll manage.'

Nodding, Mrs Shandon settled back into the seat.

Alex manoeuvred the car around a torrent that poured down one of the sandstone banks and across the road. 'Does the tractor have decent lights?'

She said, 'It has lights. I suppose they're good.'

'He'll have a trouble light, I bet,' Alex said.

Mrs Shandon said, 'Yes, of course he has. Oh, I should have taken that instead of relying on the torch—'

'A torch will pick up most things,' Alex interpolated smoothly. 'We'll take the Rover too. Where to now?'

'Turn left here. The tractor's in the big shed—the Spit paddock's about half a mile up the race.'

Ianthe was unsurprised when Alex backed the tractor out of the implement shed. Of course he'd be able to drive one, she thought ironically, adjusting the seat of the Range Rover so that she got a bit closer to the wheel. He was the sort of man who could do anything, and expected others to be able to also—like driving a Range Rover in a cyclone when you were accustomed to small city cars.

The woman beside her said defiantly, 'Rob's a good swimmer. And he's got the dogs with him.'

Mrs Shandon had to know that swimming wasn't going to help in a flooded creek, and neither were dogs, but clearly she needed whatever encouragement she could find. Easing the Range Rover into gear, Ianthe followed the huge green and yellow tractor along the metalled race that ran through the farm and towards the creek. Let him be all right, she prayed, asking for both Rob Shandon and the man driving the tractor.

They were halfway down the race when Mrs Shandon said, 'There's Bonny!'

A black and white border collie, its fur flattened to reveal its rangy body, came racing up. Ianthe slowed and Mrs Shandon wound down the window. 'Find Rob,' she shouted, her voice deadened by the rain. 'Find Rob!'

The dog hesitated, then set off towards the creek, looking periodically over its shoulder as though asking whether they were coming.

'There's a gate just here,' Mrs Shandon said abruptly.

When they came to a stop behind the tractor the older woman clambered down and ran ahead to push the gate open. Carefully Ianthe followed the tractor through, waiting while Mrs Shandon heaved the gate shut. As the small con-

voy made its way across the grass, Ianthe peered towards the turbulence that was the creek.

Usually it would be a harmless thread of water between low, scrub-covered banks. In full flood across the paddock, discoloured water tearing through teatree bushes and around hummocks of grass, it exuded danger.

The tractor stopped far closer to the water than Ianthe dared to go. Mrs Shandon hurled herself out and ran over to Alex, trailed by the dog and Ianthe. Thank heavens, she thought after three strides, this rain had come straight from the tropics, because in spite of her anorak she was already wet.

Alex was playing the trouble light—a large torch with an immensely strong beam run by the tractor battery—over the water. As the glaring light moved steadily back from the banks of the creek Mrs Shandon and Ianthe spoke together.

'There it is! There's the quad!'

Rob Shandon had clearly been within a few metres of the creek when something had tossed the quad completely over. The beam pinpointed an upturned vehicle, highlighting the four glistening circles that were the wheels. The flood waters hadn't reached it yet, but it would only be a matter of time.

Alex said, 'Something's moving—'

Another dog, black and white like Bonny, got to its feet and came out from under the quad, letting off a volley of barks, barks answered by Bonny.

'Beau,' Mrs Shandon supplied on a half-sob.

Alex shifted the light. 'Underneath,' he said sharply, holding it steady. 'That glitter—what is it?'

'Oilskins.' Ianthe's heart thudded. 'His oilskins are catching the light.'

'He's moving,' Mrs Shandon said, biting back another sob. 'Thank God.'

The light pinned the shadowed heap in its brilliant radiance. Beau struggled back to crouch beside his master.

Through the heavy curtain of rain they saw an arm lift in a feeble wave, but Rob Shandon made no attempt to rise.

'How are we going to get him back?' Ianthe asked, staring at the brown frothy torrent between them. 'Will the tractor go across?'

The older woman shook her head. 'No,' she said decisively. 'The water's running too fast and logs will start coming down any time now. Anyway, it's too deep. Rob wouldn't let you do it.'

Ianthe looked at her with enormous admiration as Alex swung the beam along the opposite bank, stopping at a post about four metres from the upturned quad.

'Could we get a loop around that?' Mrs Shandon asked tentatively.

'We'll have to.' The tractor lights revealed his frown as he gauged the width of the creek. Only forty or so feet separated them from the farmer and his dog, but the water was racing past, smoothly brown and muscular.

Ianthe said, 'You don't know what's under there—rocks, or branches…'

Adding point to her plea, for that was what it was, the jagged branch of a long-dead tree surged past, each spiky branchlet an entrapment in itself.

'I've got rope,' Alex said abruptly. 'I'll tie a loop in the middle of it, then fasten one end to the Rover and the other to the tractor so the water can't tear it out of your hands. You'll have to pay out the slack as I go across in the loop. Keep it out of the water and as taut as you can.'

Mrs Shandon stared silently at the heap of machinery under which her husband lay while Ianthe objected, 'It's too dangerous, Alex.'

'How deep is it normally?' he asked the farmer's wife.

'A metre—perhaps a bit more.'

He looked at Ianthe. 'It won't be over my head yet, and the loop will keep me safe. If I trip you can haul me upright.'

Her whole being rose in protest, but before she could

articulate the words he said, 'If he stays here all night he'll get hypothermia.'

Ianthe swung around to Mrs Shandon. 'Is there no other way of getting over there? No track through the hills?'

The older woman shook her head.

Defeated, Ianthe looked up into Alex's eyes, saw them clear and cold and hard, and knew that if anyone could help Rob Shandon he could. She didn't want to stand by and do nothing while a man died, but a primitive part of her wanted Alex kept safe.

'Some day,' she said, pitching her voice just above the roar of the flood, 'you'll have to tell me all about this childhood that saw you driving bulldozers and learning how to cross flooded rivers.'

'I'll do that,' he said with that blazing smile.

Ten minutes later she and the farmer's wife were standing well apart with a coil of rope at their feet, paying it out. The vehicles had been positioned to shine their lights over the creek and onto the upturned quad and the man beneath it.

Ianthe took what comfort she could in the knowledge that each end of the rope was tied very securely to the separate bumpers. It formed two sides of a triangle, with the women at the base angles and Alex at the apex. A loop in the middle of the length of rope was his only support in the turbulent press of water.

That, and their ability to keep the rope tight and out of the water—to work together, neither pulling too hard and jerking him off balance, nor letting the rope go too loose.

Slowly, her heart thudding, tension hollowing her stomach, Ianthe began paying out her end, holding its surprising weight steady as she tried to gauge the speed of Alex's cautious progress. It was hard work. Ignoring the rivulets of water gathering across her shoulders and the rough purchase of the rope on her hands, she looked from Mrs Shandon to Alex, trying to synchronise with the other woman so that he didn't stumble.

Please, God, she whispered silently, while Alex walked carefully, purposefully, deeper into the floodwaters.

Greedily the water rose about him, up to his waist—oh God, she thought, terrified fingers clenching as he stumbled. The loop around his chest steadied him, but it was the lithe grace she admired so much that kept him on his feet. That, and raw, stubborn strength.

Slowly he ventured further into water that came up to the middle of his chest but no higher; Ianthe could see how much effort it took him to remain on his feet, feel through the fibres of the rope the furious torrent that tried to pluck him free and toss him down the creek.

Frowning, she concentrated on easing the rope out, metre by difficult metre, keeping it tight.

Alex had chosen the place well. When at last he scrambled up the low bank, Ianthe's breath whooshed out.

Dizzily she exchanged fleeting smiles with Mrs Shandon before switching her gaze back to the other bank. Through the rain she saw Alex give a quick thumbs-up, wrench the loop above his head and drop it over the strainer post, then set off running towards the quad and its prisoner.

Almost immediately the wheels on the quad began to move, disappearing as he hauled it off the farmer, a feat of sheer, naked power that made Ianthe swallow.

He knelt beside the man; narrowing her eyes, she muttered an oath against the needles of rain that obscured her vision. Alex seemed to be taking his clothes off.

Rain stung her face, dripped through her hair, probed with increasingly chilly rivulets down her shoulders and over her breasts. Mouth tight, she stood tensely, realising that Alex was using his shirt to make some sort of sling.

There was a moment's confusion as both men got to their feet. Rob Shandon wasn't as tall as Alex but he was bigger, his thickset body further thickened by middle age. Staggering, he stood for several moments shaking his head while Alex pushed the quad further up the bank, with any luck out of the way of spreading flood waters. He rejoined the farmer, and together they picked their way across the sodden ground.

Ianthe ran back to the tractor and hauled her length of the rope around the towbar, winding it frantically so that the two men would have support against the current. It was wet and heavy, and she handled it clumsily, but fear gave her brute strength, and soon she had it as tight as she could manage it.

After a couple of half-hitches she raced over to help Mrs Shandon with the upstream length. Together the two women looped the awkward, abrasive stuff around the Rover's bumper, then turned back to the river. Bonny sidled towards them, alert, intelligent eyes fixed on Mrs Shandon's face.

'Good girl,' the older woman said, sliding her fingers over the narrow wet head. 'Good girl, Bonny. Sit, now.'

Tensely they watched as the two men reached the downstream length of the now taut rope. After they'd ducked under, Alex guided his companion's right hand to it and the two men began the slow trip back. Eyes drowned with sudden tears, the older woman said jaggedly, 'I don't know who he is, but he's got guts and a good brain, and I'm going to be grateful to him for the rest of my life.'

Both women gasped when Rob stumbled, clutching at the lifeline as Alex's strong hands on his belt dragged him upright. Left behind, Beau ran up and down the bank before following the men into the water. The stream took him and carried him off, but he was swimming vigorously, head held high.

'He'll be all right,' Mrs Shandon said at Ianthe's murmur of concern. 'He'll come ashore like Bonny.'

Ianthe nodded, almost running to the edge of the stream, hand pressed over her mouth to stifle a shout as the farmer staggered again and this time almost went under. Once more Alex yanked him upright.

She yelled a warning as a branch hurtled down. Immediately Alex positioned himself to deflect it with his shoulder and upper arm. It went past without hitting them, but she muttered urgently, 'Hurry up! Get out of there!'

The two men inched forward with excruciating care. In the glare of the headlights she saw the farmer's face, pale with pain and hypothermia, and now she could see that Alex's shirt tied one arm to his body.

Ianthe heard Mrs Shandon say, 'Good dog, Beau,' and realised that the second dog had made it across, but she couldn't take her eyes off the men, one staggering and almost spent, the other still with reserves to call on.

Then they were only two steps away. And Rob Shandon tripped a third time, taking Alex with him.

'No!' Ianthe pushed into the roiling waters, one hand on the taut rope, the other groping for Rob Shandon. Fingers clenching in his hair, she dragged his head up out of the water and with his wife's help hauled him by his good shoulder and the collar of his shirt far enough out of the creek so that he could breathe.

Heart in her mouth, Ianthe swung around, but Alex was already getting to his feet, his chest heaving as he coughed. Water ran off his torso in sheets, emphasising the strong muscles beneath the sleek skin.

'Here,' she croaked, holding out her hand.

He laughed, his face alight with fierce exultation. 'You're in the water,' he said, and grabbed her hand.

The current tore at her feet and legs, snatching her off balance as Alex pulled her against him, shielding her from the full force of the flow. Although he was breathing heavily, his eyes glittered with triumph. Ianthe stood with water surging insistently around her and felt nothing but an immense relief, because Alex was safe.

'Yes,' she said, and hand in hand they scrambled up the bank. Laughing, suddenly light-headed, Ianthe hugged the man beside her, and his mouth came down in a kiss that wiped out everything but a glorious, singing delight.

A labouring but amused voice put an end to that kiss.

'Some people,' Rob Shandon observed, slurring the words, 'don't have the sense to come in out of the rain.'

Alex lifted his head and grinned. 'I believe you,' he said drily, setting Ianthe to one side.

While Mrs Shandon checked his head her husband smiled, in spite of the dusky swelling across his cheekbone, and the hypothermia that had to be well set in by now.

'Let's get you back to the house,' Alex commanded. He looked at Ianthe. 'You take the Shandons, I'll bring the tractor.'

'You're too cold,' she protested. 'Come back in the Rover—it's got a heater.'

'No. If we leave the tractor here the flood might wash it away.'

Back at the farmhouse the power was off, but Mrs Shandon organised her small troop of helpers with efficiency and dispatch. As she and Alex supported her husband into the bedroom she looked over her shoulder at Ianthe who, shivering and feeling the after-effects of an adrenalin rush, was guiding them with a torch.

'Can you leave that one here and get the little torch by the bed and find your way into the laundry?' she said. 'There are two gas lamps there and a gas element in the bottom middle cupboard. Do you know how to light them?'

'Yes.'

'Good. We'll need hot water, so start heating some. The saucepans are in the cupboard beside the sink.'

'And get out of those clothes,' Alex said, frowning as he looked at Ianthe.

'I'm the least affected of you all,' she said briskly, snatching up the bedside torch after she'd put the big one on the dressing table so that the beam illuminated the bed.

'No, he's right. Take what you want from the pile of ironing on the board in the laundry,' Mrs Shandon said. 'And some towels. Rub yourself down. Careful, Rob, we're nearly there, love. And there are at least three hot water bottles in the bottom cupboard in the laundry too. Fill them as soon as possible.'

Ianthe found the lamps, lit them, and took one into the bedroom where Alex and Mrs Shandon were stripping the clothes from her husband. There was no sign of amusement on his face now; although she'd set the heater on high in the Range Rover shock had truly set in, and it didn't need his harsh breathing or the shudders that shook his big frame to tell her that the sooner he was in bed surrounded by hot water bottles the better it would be.

Back in the large, dim kitchen, Ianthe lit the gas element and set a pan of water on it, then struggled free of the clinging embrace of her wet clothes and towelled down, shivering as she gratefully got into a sweatshirt and skirt. She felt strange without any underclothes, but wearing her own soaked bra and pants would rob her of precious heat.

The singing of the water in the saucepan changed note, so she raced across and carefully, because her hands were stiff and clumsy, tipped it into a hot water bottle.

A movement in the doorway jerked her head around. Silently, somehow looming in the yellow light of the lamp, Alex came into the room. The light slid off his bare torso in copper slabs.

A pulse beat in her throat, but he was shivering, and as she refilled the pan she said, 'You should change your clothes.'

'That's what I'm planning to do,' he said, frowning. 'Where's that torch?'

She picked it up from the bench and gave it to him. His hands were cold, but not icy. Relieved, she said, 'I'll take the hot water bottle in to Mr Shandon.'

She only stayed a moment, because the farmer was propped up in the bed, pale and drawn, with his eyes closed and his mouth a taut line of pain.

Back in the kitchen, Ianthe listened to the rain drumming on the corrugated iron roof, drowning out every other sound but the low, rough noise that Rob Shandon made as his wife set his arm. Gritting her teeth, Ianthe willed the water to heat faster.

From what she could remember of her first aid training, in hypothermia the first priority was to get the patient warm, especially on this occasion as he was in shock from the broken arm. Thank heavens Mrs Shandon was a nurse.

Brows drawn together, Alex came back through the door.

Although the shirt and jeans were too short in the arms and legs, and too big, his innate male elegance overwhelmed any incongruity. He should have looked exhausted, but his energy and vitality overcame his tiredness.

'Is everything all right?' Ianthe demanded, more sharply than she'd intended.

The frown disappeared. 'Yes, he's fine,' he said. 'Still in a lot of pain, of course, but if we can get him warm he'll be all right.'

'Will three hot water bottles do?'

'If that's all there are, they'll have to,' he said.

'You still look cold,' she said, voicing her concern in the only way she could.

'Don't worry about me. I'm tougher than I look.'

Not likely, she thought, making the mistake of glancing up at him. Her stomach performed one of its more complicated gymnastic turns. He looked—satisfied, light eyes gleaming, his mouth curled in a smile. And he looked tough, with more than the sheer physical courage he'd shown as he made his way across that creek—a deeper kind of courage altogether. He was a man who wouldn't break.

Unlike her. She'd allowed herself to be shattered by a stupid phobia. Did her step into the flooded creek mean an end to that? Oh, she hoped so.

Forcing her voice into a flat, prosaic timbre, she asked, 'Are you still shivering?'

'No. I'm all right, Ianthe, don't fuss.'

She grabbed the second hot water bottle and filled it. Lean fingers took the bottle from hers, and kept her in place by clasping her wrist. 'How are you?' he demanded.

'Not a shiver.' She didn't dare look up because her husky reply gave her away. 'The rain's warm enough, and I didn't go right into the creek.'

'It wasn't too bad,' Alex said as he turned her wrist. 'I haven't got any of the signs of hypothermia.'

Certainly his colour was back to normal—no sign of the pale line around his mouth.

He said in an altered voice, 'You've got blisters.'

'It was the rope,' she said unevenly.

Her heart stopped as he lifted her hand and kissed the small swellings. 'You did really well,' he said against her skin.

'Mrs Shandon and I did well,' she said, the words echoing around her empty brain.

'You don't panic,' he said. 'It's a rare quality.' And he let her go and walked out of the room.

Ianthe stood for a moment with her blistered palms pressed against her hot cheeks, then got on with her tasks.

An hour later she took tea in to Mrs Shandon, sitting beside her dozing husband, and went back to drink hers in the kitchen with Alex. Beyond thanking her for it, he said little. The barriers had been reimposed; his face was controlled and withdrawn, its deliberate detachment effectively warding off any attempt at communication.

After she'd made them sandwiches, and insisted they eat them, Alex suggested that they take it in turns to watch the sleeping man. When Mrs Shandon objected he said gently, 'We don't know how long the road is going to be cut off, so you need some rest.'

Mrs Shandon said, 'I'll get into bed with Rob and warm him—I can doze then.'

'Wake me in four hours, or if you want help,' Alex said.

It wasn't exactly an order, but in spite of her fears for her husband the older woman smiled. 'Or you'll know the reason why?' she said. 'All right, I'll do that.'

Ianthe said crisply, 'Don't wake him, wake me.' She traded glances with Alex. 'You,' she pointed out, 'have done your bit for the night. You need to warm up too, and you certainly need to sleep. You must be exhausted.'

Mrs Shandon looked amused. Before Alex could speak she said, 'She's right, you know. I'll wake her.'

The heavy lids of Alex's eyes lifted. Transferring his gaze to his hostess, he smiled. With resignation Ianthe watched the older woman reel back. That smile, she thought, should be packaged and sold; it would make him millions as an explosive alone.

'Very well,' he said.

Mrs Shandon looked at her watch. 'It's only ten o'clock,' she said in wonder. 'It feels as though we spent all damned night on that bank.'

Ianthe asked, 'Are you all right?'

'Yes,' the older woman said simply. 'Just grateful that you two were there. I'd never have got across the creek, let alone been able to lift the quad off Rob.'

'You'd have managed,' Alex said. 'It's amazing what you can do when the life of someone you love is at stake.'

Mrs Shandon smiled. 'I know, I've seen some astounding things, but we're talking miracles here. You two were ours, Rob's and mine. Now, off you both go and get some sleep.'

They chose bedrooms next to each other, rooms that had once belonged to the Shandon children. At the door to Ianthe's Alex said, 'Are you warm enough?'

'I'm fine,' she said automatically. 'What about you? We can heat up enough water for you to wash in.'

'It's not necessary,' he said dismissively. 'Unlike Rob, I don't have hypothermia.'

'You courted it, going back out into the rain to feed and dry the dogs.' She sounded abrupt, as though she had the right to be concerned.

'They deserved it,' he said. He looked at her in the lamp-lit dimness of the narrow hall, its papered walls dotted with small bunches of flowers, and suddenly her breath stilled in her throat.

Hastily, because the silence was too intimate and she

didn't know how to put a graceful stop to it, she said, 'Rescuing Rob was—very heroic.'

He shrugged. 'You'd have done it if I wasn't there.'

'I doubt it,' she said. 'I hadn't realised how unfit I am.'

Her leg was aching, but not too badly. Adrenalin, she thought grimly, was a wonderful hormone. Tomorrow her arms and shoulders would hurt. Once more she was exasperated because she'd let the shark attack turn her into a wimp.

'Hospital does that to you,' he said, but aloofly, as though he was thinking of something else.

She said, 'Goodnight.'

'Goodnight.'

Ianthe turned and slipped in through the door, aware that if she stayed she was going to do something stupid, like hold up her face for a kiss.

Fortunately her watch had an alarm. She set it for two hours, pulled off the skirt she was wearing and got into the bed, willing herself to sleep.

When the tinny beep persisted she could have killed it, but crawled out of bed, hesitated a moment before deciding not to struggle back into the skirt, and then, bare-legged and shivering slightly, found her way to the door. Although the rain had eased, gusts of wind were pouncing on the house, rattling a window somewhere before rushing on. A thin sliver of light shone beneath the main bedroom door. She hesitated again, then continued on to the kitchen and groped for the small gadget that set the gas ring alight, smiling when her fingers brushed it exactly where she'd been careful to leave it before she'd gone to bed. Once the jets were flaring, she used their glow to fill a pan of water and set it onto the element.

'Ianthe?' Alex's quiet voice made her jump.

'Over here,' she said, her throat strained.

He closed the door behind him and came across the room. 'Can't you sleep?'

'I thought I'd refill the hot water bottles.'

He was silent for a moment, then said, 'I'll do it next time.'

'You don't need to,' she said, moving away slightly because he was too close.

'I believe in equality,' he said, that note of amusement back in his deep voice. 'I'll go and collect a bottle now.'

He was back in a few minutes.

'How is he?' Ianthe asked.

'His breathing's still bad but he's warming up. I'm glad his wife knows what to do.' He spoke almost absently, and when she glanced up she saw that he was looking at her legs, indistinctly outlined by the soft, warm glow of the gas ring.

Her first instinct was to move, to shield the scar from his eyes, but she stood still. He'd seen it before. Besides, he wasn't looking at the scar. Transfixed, she waited while that splintering gaze travelled upwards, touching off explosions of honeyed fire deep in the hidden places of her body. Sexuality, bold and predatory, smouldered in the clear pale depths of his eyes.

Heat stole through Ianthe, colouring her skin. Her eyes widened, became heavy-lidded, drowsy with desire and invitation. Alex was watching her with half-lowered eyelids, sending delicious shivers through her.

'You look like a sea nymph,' he said, the words rough and blunt. 'I promised myself I wouldn't touch you, wouldn't let you get to me, but it was too late the first time I saw you. You stood in that room and lifted your chin, and I saw the bruises Mark had made on your wrist and I wanted to kill him.'

Bewildered, shocked, Ianthe shook her head, and he laughed softly, humourlessly, his mouth hardening as he reined in his emotions.

'The water must be hot enough, surely.' Alex's harsh words echoed like shards around her head.

'Almost,' she muttered, reaching for the water bottle.

Slowly, stretching her aching body, Ianthe woke. The steady thrumming of the rain on the corrugated iron roof had diminished to a soft patter, and through it she could hear a loud morning chorus of birdsong.

A swift glance at her watch shot her out of bed. Pulling on the skirt she'd borrowed, she ran along the hall. She was about to knock on the bedroom door when Mrs Shandon opened it, yawning and rubbing sleep from her eyes.

'How is he?' Ianthe asked, but with no urgency this time.

The answer was in Mrs Shandon's face. Her smile wasn't entirely free from worry, but there was none of the controlled fear of the previous night. 'Feverish and in pain, but he'll make it, although I hope the road's cleared so we can get him to hospital. Do you want a cup of tea?'

'I'd love one.'

Mrs Shandon closed the door behind her and walked with Ianthe along the passage. 'Thank you for everything you've done.'

'It was nothing. Did you get any sleep?'

Her hostess led the way into the kitchen. As she put the electric kettle on she said with a smile, 'I did a lot of dozing. The power came on about four-thirty this morning, and by then Rob was breathing much more easily and his temperature was normal, so I got up and washed your clothes and put them in the drier before trundling back to bed. After that I slept like a rock. If you want to iron your clothes they'll still be in the drier.'

'Oh, thank you,' Ianthe said gratefully. 'Is your farm a dairy farm, like the others along the road?'

'No, we changed to beef last year. Have you been worrying about the cows?'

'Well, I thought someone should milk them.'

'Fortunately the beef stock don't need it.'

After they'd drunk their tea Ianthe slipped into her clean underclothes and began to iron her clothes. She'd finished and pulled trousers and shirt on when the hair on the back of her neck lifted. She looked over her shoulder.

Alex stood in the doorway, clad only in the trousers he'd worn the previous night, and with a villainously shadowed jaw. 'Good morning,' he said in a rasping, just woken voice.

'Hi.' Dragging her gaze away from the bronze expanse of chest and the smooth, supple width of his torso, she said with all the composure she could muster, 'Mrs Shandon's tried the telephone and it's still down. Did you bring your cellphone? We need to find out if the road's open.'

He nodded. It hadn't worried Ianthe that Mrs Shandon had seen her tangled hair, but she was acutely conscious of it now.

'It's still in the Rover,' he said. 'I'll go and ring the emergency services, but they're not going to be able to clear the road with just a grader. It will have to be a bull-dozer, and as they're probably all being used in Dargaville to keep the Wairoa River banks in order, we may have to get a chopper in.'

'Would you like me to iron your clothes while you ring?' she asked, smiling, trying to sound casual. 'Mrs Shandon washed and dried them last night when the power came back on.'

When he spoke it was slowly, as though he wasn't think-ing about what he was saying. 'No, I'll do it.'

Miserably aware of her limp, Ianthe fled.

Five minutes later, face washed and her hair finger-combed, she was on her way to the kitchen when she heard voices from the laundry. She hesitated, then followed them. Alex was standing to one side looking amused while his hostess wielded the iron with the skill of long years spent behind one. 'He wants to see you,' she was saying, and turned her head to include Ianthe. 'Both of you. When you're ready, of course.'

'Alex,' Ianthe accused, 'you told me you were going to iron your own clothes.'

He grinned. 'I was—'

'Badly,' interrupted Mrs Shandon, smiling. 'I don't suppose you've had to iron anything before in your life.'

'You're wrong,' he said promptly. 'I used to be an expert, but I must admit it's been a long time, and clearly it's the sort of skill you need to keep practising.'

'There,' Mrs Shandon said, pulling the shirt from the ironing board in one smooth motion and handing it over. 'If you wait a moment I'll have the trousers done.'

He shrugged into the shirt and buttoned it up, his eyes gleaming. 'You've gone down in Ianthe's estimation,' he said. 'She thinks you should let me do my own.'

'It would be better for your character,' Ianthe told him briskly, feeling oddly shut out.

'I expect his character is well and truly formed by now,' their hostess remarked, pressing in the creases with an experienced hand. 'Here you are. I'll get us breakfast.'

'I'll see if I can raise Civil Defence again,' Alex said.

Mrs Shandon switched off the iron and turned a wavering smile on him. 'Go and see Rob first, will you?' she asked.

What began as an awkward interview was made much easier by Alex's tact. If asked, Ianthe would have said that the two men could have had nothing in common, yet within minutes she realised that the farmer liked and respected the man who'd rescued him, a feeling returned by Alex.

'We all helped,' Alex said. 'Tell me, had you managed to move the cattle before you got flipped?'

'Yes.' He frowned. 'I don't even know what happened, you know. I can't remember.'

'That's what a knock on the head does,' Alex said.

'You don't need a knock; shock will do it,' Ianthe said. She barely remembered being attacked by the shark; she'd seen film of it, so she knew what had happened, but the incident itself was almost wiped from her brain. Sometimes she thought she might have dealt with it more effectively had she been able to recall it.

Alex sent her a piercing glance which she held. He nodded, and returned to Rob. 'Don't worry,' he said. 'If you're safe and your stock's safe that's all that matters.'

'And the dogs,' Ianthe reminded him.

Laughter glimmered in Alex's eyes as Rob Shandon said, 'Yes, by God!'

CHAPTER SEVEN

THE road was still closed.

'Helicopter it is,' Alex said, and spoke concisely to the person on the other end of the cellphone.

Yes, this was the man who'd single-handedly built a huge corporation. Authority crackled through his voice, and when the other person made some sort of demur he said inflexibly, 'That won't do. He needs to get to hospital as soon as possible.'

It was enough. He listened and said, 'Yes. We'll expect it.' Putting the cellphone away, he said, 'They'll be here in half an hour.'

Seated beside her husband, Mrs Shandon listened to the arrangements and nodded. 'I'll have to stay,' she said calmly. 'Someone has to look after the stock.'

Alex asked, 'Will you be able to do that if you can't drive the tractor?'

'I can check them and move them around the paddocks with the dogs; Rob's given me a list of where they're to go.' She looked at her husband and warned, 'And no bribing the chopper pilot to come back early, do you hear? They'll have the grader here by tomorrow morning at the latest, and I can manage until then. If the worst comes to the worst I'll ask Alex and Ianthe for help again.'

Rob grunted, but appeared to accept that he'd be confined to hospital for at least one night. 'What about our car?' he asked.

'We'll bring it back,' Alex said. 'In fact, we can do that now.'

It was a silent journey to the house by the lake. The knowledge that this really was the end—once the road was

114

open he'd take her home and she'd never see him again—pressed heavily on Ianthe, and Alex seemed to have nothing to say.

She drove the Rover back to the farmhouse while Alex followed in the Shandons' car. As she turned in the farm gate she heard the noisy thump of a helicopter's rotors coming in low and fast.

After they'd waved Rob off they drank a final cup of tea together. Mrs Shandon thanked them, assured Alex that she'd ask if she needed any help, and thanked them again.

Back in the Range Rover, Ianthe hesitated to break into the charged atmosphere. He'd retreated inside himself, his hard-edged features grim and withdrawn. When they turned down the drive towards the lake she asked, 'Would the Rover cope with the forestry roads in the plantation?'

'No, those tracks will be impassable until tomorrow at the earliest. You'll have to wait until the road's cleared before you'll be able to get back home.'

Ianthe nodded, hoping that the road would be open soon.

Some time during the previous twenty-four hours her emotions had taken a giant step into the unknown. Until yesterday she'd convinced herself that the emotions roiling through her had been no more than a strong sexual attraction, the heated hunger caused by hormones and physical need.

But after talking to him the previous evening, after watching him laugh with Mrs Shandon, after his perilous trek across the flooded creek and the incandescent glory of the kiss that followed it, after hearing his flat, harshly spoken words in the middle of the night, and seeing him unshaven and bare-chested in the early-morning light, she no longer knew what she felt.

Attraction was simple to deal with. Ignore it, starve it, and eventually it died. Love—that complex mixture of emotions and desire, of needs and promise and hope, of passion and respect and liking—oh, love was a much more difficult proposition.

It still wasn't too late, she comforted herself as they drew in under the *porte-cochère*. She'd never forget Alex, but when he left she'd get over it.

Ignoring the twist of pain in her heart, she opened the door and climbed down. To support her aching leg she leaned for a moment against the door and stared up into the sky. The heavy pall of cloud was moving, thinning, breaking up.

Grateful for a neutral subject, Ianthe said, 'We got off lightly this time. I wonder if the cyclone caused any damage further south.'

He looked at his watch. 'We should catch the news on the radio.'

The smooth-voiced newsreader told them there had been minor flooding, but with the unpredictability that cyclones were famous for this storm had swung away into the chilly reaches of the Tasman Sea and filled in rapidly, its powerhouse of energy swiftly shattered by the cool currents welling up from the Antarctic.

'That's a relief—' Ianthe began to say.

'Quiet!'

Startled, she stared at him. His brows knotted as the announcer went on, 'The army has been drawn into the situation in Illyria, where for the past three weeks thousands of citizens have been marching in silent protest at the present administration. Heavy gunfire has been heard around the city, and all foreigners have been ordered to leave.'

Alex leaned down and switched off the radio. 'Would you like a cup of coffee?'

'Not just now, thank you.' Ianthe hesitated. The dark, autocratic face hadn't altered, but she sensed a seething turmoil of emotions behind his composure, and the ice in his eyes had turned to steel. 'You said that your family in Illyria are all dead, but do you still know people there?'

He gave her a fierce glance, sharp as a stiletto. 'Why do you ask?' Again that hint of an accent, so faint it was less than an intonation.

'You seem to have a very personal interest in what's going on there.'

He said nothing. Outside a gull gave a long, wailing cry, falling into a silence that echoed around and through Ianthe, chilling her to the bones.

Finally he said, 'I am Illyrian.' Her mouth opened but she said nothing, and his polished eyes narrowed. 'Hadn't you guessed?'

'No.' She said foolishly, 'I thought you were Italian.'

'I grew up in Illyria in a small mountain village until I was ten; when my father was taken by the communists my mother and I had to flee. We ended up in Australia.'

She wanted to know more, but a sudden terror struck her. 'You're not going back, are you?' she asked quietly.

Another silence. Her heart skidded into a slow pounding, echoing through her ears. She stared at him, seeing a different man. Although the dynamic power beneath the urbane surface had always been obvious, until then it had been diffused. Now it was directed, his energy honed and channelled to a purpose, the overwhelming drive harnessed. He was leaving to fulfil a destiny in which she had no part.

'Alex,' she said, reaching out to him, no longer able to control her emotions. 'Alex, there's going to be a war there.'

'I might be able to stop it,' he said.

She grabbed his wrist, shaking it. 'You can't—you're only one man! Oh, you've got power and money, but it's going to be a civil war and you could get killed!'

His hand closed over hers. 'I don't think so,' he said, and as she opened her mouth he said harshly, 'I have to go.'

'You're not responsible for them,' she objected with fierce intensity.

His eyes bored into hers, inimical, uncompromising. 'I am,' he said simply.

She exhaled a sharp, hissing breath. The words wouldn't come, and he said nothing, made no attempt to help her as

she stared at him, appalled at her sudden leap of intuition.
'You're the lost p-prince,' she stammered. 'Aren't you?'

'I'm his son. I hope he's dead.' He looked at her white,
shocked face and said harshly, 'If he isn't, he's been in a
communist prison for the past twenty-four years.'

Ianthe dragged her hand away from his wrist as though
the skin and tendons and bones were red-hot. 'But the communists were overthrown three years ago. Surely the prisoners were released—'

'No. When the junta came into power they said there
were no political prisoners. A situation they've remedied—
the gaols are full of them now.'

She took a deep, impeded breath and whispered, 'They'll
kill you if you go back.'

'Why should they? Like you, neither the communists before nor the junta now believe I can have any interest in
Illyria—after all, I have more power, more wealth than they
can ever aspire to. What on earth would lure me back to a
small, unstable, impoverished country?' His smile was a
harsh, unamused accompaniment to words that echoed with
a cold, cutting cynicism. 'If I'd been in any danger I'd have
been threatened by now. I've never told anyone who I am,
but I look like my father, and our family name is Considine.
Those in power have probably always known who I am,
and now the ordinary people have heard rumours that a
Considine is still alive. That's why they're marching, why
I feel responsible for them. Anyway, I'm not going back
to claim the throne.' His mouth twisted. 'God knows, I
don't want that sort of power. But when the communists
took over thousands of people died appalling deaths, and if
something isn't done soon thousands more could be killed
in a squalid, useless civil war. I might be able to stop any
more bloodshed.'

'How?'

He shrugged and turned away. 'I've been contacted by
various people, influential people who've never given up
hope that one day a Considine might come back to take

over the throne. They believe that by virtue of my ancestry I'll have some sort of moral sway over the people. The army is the key; they stay with the junta because they can see no other prospect of peace. If I go back the generals might just be persuaded to send the junta on its way and help the people form some sort of democratic government.'

'Or the junta might kill you,' she said furiously.

'It's highly unlikely.'

'For heaven's sake, these people are trying to cling to power. Just because you're rich and powerful and famous doesn't make you armour-plated, you know. Bullets kill tycoons as well as ord—'

He put his hand over her mouth, stopping the angry, frightened words. Ianthe wrenched herself away, fighting for control, her eyes glazed with tears.

Very quietly, Alex said, 'I have to go, Ianthe.'

She bit her lip. 'I have no right to try and stop you,' she said stiffly, the words aching in her throat, heavy with unshed tears.

He said, 'I owe them this, at least, to try and stop the sort of carnage you see on your television screen every night. What sort of man would I be if I stayed away and let it happen?'

'Sensible,' she said, the word wrenched from deep within her.

'But not honourable.' He was ruthless, and she could see that she had no power to change his mind.

She sighed. 'No, and not responsible, either. And that's your big thing, responsibility.'

He shrugged, suddenly alien to her. 'It's the way I was brought up,' he said calmly. 'Are you hungry?'

Surprised, Ianthe said, 'No. What time is it?'

'Almost one o'clock. We'll eat lunch, then I'll see if the road is clear enough for the Rover to get past.'

Then he'd take her back to the bach and say goodbye, and she'd never see him again.

Unless it was on television…

In the modern kitchen with its granite bench and luxurious efficiency Ianthe made pasta, and Alex tossed a salad and found fruit.

She had no appetite, but to please him she picked at the food out on the terrace, watching the water return to its normal colour as the clouds slowly dissipated and the sun burst through. A solid, heavy lump had lodged halfway down her throat. While they drank coffee the telephone rang.

Frowning, Alex picked it up. 'Mark? How are things there?' He listened, then said, 'Make sure your sister doesn't need you.'

Apparently she didn't, because he'd be back as soon as the roads were clear.

Deliberately Ianthe relaxed her facial muscles. The tension was beginning to tell on her, and she sensed a controlled restlessness in Alex. He couldn't wait to be rid of her.

To get herself out of the room she said quietly, 'My leg's aching. I'll lie down until it stops.'

'Of course. Do you want a painkiller?' His voice was cool, edged with an unknown emotion.

'No, it will soon ease.'

Your heart doesn't really break, Ianthe reminded herself as she walked into the bedroom. You've mourned before and recovered from it. It's mainly frustration, anyway, because you want him and you know it's not going to happen.

Nothing was going to happen—not now, not ever—yet she'd never forget Alex.

And he wasn't going to get killed in that small principality on the other side of the world. Fate wouldn't be so unkind.

Shivering in the sticky heat, she pulled back the coverlet, took off her shoes and her trousers and shirt, got onto the big, comfortable bed, and closed her eyes. Of course she wouldn't sleep. Inevitably, she began to go over every moment since she'd met Alex, every word he'd said, every expression she'd deciphered, the times he'd kissed her. And as drowsiness claimed her, she made a bargain with the future. She wouldn't cling, wouldn't tell him that she'd somehow managed to fall in love with him, she wouldn't cry or grieve, if only he stayed alive. That was all she asked.

She woke to a knock on the door and Alex's voice. Disoriented, bewildered, she struggled upright on the pillow and croaked out, 'Come in.'

Alex walked in through the door, then stopped, his eyes kindling. A wild excitement pumped through Ianthe. She'd forgotten that she was lying on the bed with only her bra and her pants on. And during the sleep she hadn't expected she'd managed to kick the coverlet off.

She should drag it above her breasts, hide herself from the pale fire of Alex's gaze, get out of his house as fast as she could. Because they had no future. His destiny lay far distant from hers. Yet the drugging, languorous aftermath of sleep, and a seething rebellion because she was never going to see him again, held her still.

'Alex?' she said, her husky voice filled with longing.

He closed his eyes, but opened them immediately, and the naked hunger burning beneath the thick lashes sent her senses into overdrive. In a raw, constricted voice he said, 'You are so beautiful.'

It was almost an accusation.

She shook her head. '*You* are beautiful,' she said simply, adding, 'The most beautiful man I've ever seen.'

His lean hands clenched into fists. Tautly, each word brittle and fierce, he said, 'This is not sensible, Ianthe.'

'I know,' she said, swallowing the lump in her throat.

'God, I can cope with almost anything but sadness!' He came across to the bed in several swift, silent steps and sat down on the edge. His hand trembled as he touched her mouth.

The simple gesture seared through her, setting her inhibitions afire, burning them away. She put up a hand and held his against her lips, her eyes meeting his with a shy, resolute urgency.

The pupils darkened as his eyes dilated, and in them was a white-hot urgency that sent an elemental pleasure sizzling through her, smashing all the sensible barriers of common sense and prudence and decorum.

This, at least, she would have. Caution sometimes exacted too high a price. Reaching out, she touched the rough silk of his cheek, feeling her fingers tremble against the heated skin.

Who made the last, irrevocable move she never knew— whether she offered first, or he took—but he bore her down onto the bed and kissed her with such famished passion that she surrendered immediately, opening her mouth to his unfettered desire, turning wild at the taste of him, the faint, potent scent of aroused male, the consuming need that roared through every cell in her body with the awesome speed and power and beauty of a bushfire.

And its danger.

Her hands clung to his shoulders, pulling him closer and closer so that she could feel his precious weight, and she gasped when he kissed her throat and the soft, swelling mounds of her breasts.

'Alex,' she breathed, her voice lazy with promise, fierce with desire, a primitive invitation to delights beyond bearing, rapture too great to endure.

'Your hair's like sunlight,' he said, his voice raw and relentless. 'It's the first thing I noticed about you—such thick, sunlit masses of it, with hidden, fiery streaks the colour of untarnished copper. I wanted you then...'

He spread it back on the pillow and buried his face in it. I'll never cut it again, Ianthe thought dazedly.

Lifting his head, he ran a lingering, possessive hand across her breasts, finding the indentation of her waist, caressing the little hollow of her navel, the jut of her hip and the silken skin at the top of her thigh.

Ianthe's breath lodged in her throat. She longed for the more intimate touch of his hand; mesmerised, her whole body aching and tense, she couldn't stop the twist of her hips, the sudden, betraying thrust against his hand.

And he jackknifed off the bed, his eyes bleak, and said harshly, 'No!'

The brutal rejection seared through her, reducing the blossoming flower of her sensuality to a husk. Hastily, with clumsy shaking fingers, she twitched the coverlet across her legs, hiding the scar, and up to her shoulders. She couldn't meet his eyes; longing for him to get out and leave her to deal with her humiliation alone, she turned her head and fixed her gaze on the trees outside the window.

'It's not your leg,' he said, the words hard-edged.

'Don't worry about it.' Her voice was thin and brisk. 'I know it's ugly. I'm having plastic surgery on it next year, but there'll always be a scar. It's all right.'

In one smooth movement he yanked back the cover. Ianthe closed her eyes. So lightly she could barely feel it, he stroked from her thigh to just above the ankle with cool, steady fingers. She shuddered, feeling his touch strum through her like the vibrations of a guitar string, setting off a shattering response.

'It isn't all right,' he said inflexibly. 'Look at me.'

What the hell did he want—blood? Her heart's essence, so he could spurn it?

'Look at me,' he repeated, and this time it was a command, delivered with soft ruthlessness, a dangerous, compelling insistence.

She turned her head and lifted her lashes. Sculpted in bronze, his face was an unyielding mask cast in lines of disturbing aggression.

In a quiet, chilling voice he said, 'Any man who's repelled by that scar doesn't deserve you. You're liquid fire in the sunlight, with honey in your voice and a laugh warm enough to heat ice to steam.'

Oh, she wanted to believe him. Her eyes fell, to see his

hand, tanned and graceful against the shiny skin of her scar. 'Then why did you—did you pull away from me?' she whispered, her need to know more important than any humiliation.

The blue clarity of his eyes darkened as his mouth tightened. 'I'm not going to make love with you like some soldier going off to war, greedily taking pleasure in case it's the last time. I can't offer you anything.' The words were cold and precise, so distinct they were like whips across her heart. 'Not a future—hell, I can't even offer you a present. I'm leaving New Zealand later tonight.'

This was what it was like to have your heart ripped to shreds. Oh, common sense had warned her that nothing could come of the attraction that flamed between them, but she had hoped—and now there was bitter sorrow where those secret hopes had been hiding.

'It's all right,' she said again, knowing she must sound inane yet unable to think of any other words. 'Alex, don't worry. I understand.'

He began to speak, and then stopped. Ianthe heard her heartbeat, quick, shuddering in rhythm with her uneven breathing. I can't bear this, she thought desperately.

'Alex,' she said, damping down every emotion because that was the only way she could function, 'I find you very attractive, but we don't know each other—' her voice faltered, then firmed '—not at all, really.'

'So it's going to be easy to forget?' he said cynically. 'I hope so. I won't make love with you, Ianthe, because you deserve more than I can give you.'

He got up from the bed and walked across the room. Standing like a shadow in the doorway, he said without emphasis, 'But never think I don't want you. I do. More than I've ever wanted anyone else. Rather more than I ever *will* want anyone else, I'm afraid.'

He opened the door and went out, closing it noiselessly behind him. Ianthe huddled against the pillows, her pulses beating raggedly. Oh, he had meant that. The authentic note of passion had lit each word with fire, with hunger beyond understanding, and she crouched and hugged herself, rocking back and forth and longing for tears, because that admission was all she was ever going to get from Alex.

But she couldn't give way to grief here.

Hastily, numbly, she got up and showered and dressed. She would, she thought mordantly, rather face that shark again than go into the sitting room and say goodbye to Alex, but she was going to have to do it. The only consolation was that she'd be going home soon.

Setting her chin, and only too aware of the smudges under her eyes and the tired pallor of her skin, she walked into the living room.

Alex was standing just outside on the terrace, staring out across the water, but when she came into the room he swung around, his eyes narrowing as he surveyed her face.

'The road's clear,' he said.

Her lips felt stiff, as though they'd never be able to curve upwards again. 'So I can go back to the bach.' Her voice sounded husky and flat.

'Yes.'

They drove through the drenched countryside, making an occasional comment about the pools of water that lay on the sodden paddocks, the branches tumbled on the ground in a litter of twigs and leaves. A kilometre or so past Alex's gate new layers of sandstone bank had fallen away, spattering boulders and slush across the recently graded surface.

'Stay there,' Alex said, opening the door and striding around behind the vehicle, to reappear with a shovel.

He swung it as if part of him found a savage pleasure in the physical activity. Ianthe watched his muscles move beneath the thin cotton shirt, the steady, powerful grace as he threw each shovel-load to the side of the road, the angular, hawk-like profile burning darkly against the pale bank, and she ached with hunger—and something more fierce that came from the depths of her soul.

'Sorry, I'm a bit wet,' he said as he got back in.

'Not to worry.'

The bach was in perfect condition, although the macrocarpa tree had been battered into ruin. Alex frowned up at the tangle of dark needles and twisted branches. 'Get someone in to look at it before tonight.'

'Yes.'

He stayed until he was satisfied that everything in the building worked, then stood just inside the door and looked at her. His eyes were cool and depthless, his mouth compressed, the chiselled features etched more sharply.

'Goodbye,' he said. 'Promise me something, will you?'

She would have promised him the world. 'What?'

'That you'll keep trying to get back in the water.'

'Yes, all right,' she said, listening to the sound of her heart breaking.

'I've seen a video of one of your documentaries and you were born for the water. And you'll make it. Swim for me. Dive through that wall of blue.'

She swallowed to ease the painful knot of tears clogging her throat and nodded, and turned away as he walked out through the door. Her hands clenched on the verandah railing; she stood staring sightlessly at the lake as the Range Rover started up and drove away.

Tricia had rung the store, leaving an urgent message, so later that afternoon Ianthe contacted her.

'Are you all right?' Tricia demanded.

'Yes, I'm fine, and so's the bach.'

'Oh, blast the bach! I nearly had a fit when I rang your father's place and found out you were still there. Listen, do you want to come and stay for a while with me?'

'No, idiot! I'm fine.' Her voice sounded shrill, almost rasping, and she softened it to say, 'The bach is in really good shape, but the macrocarpa is a mess.'

Tricia listened as she detailed the damage, then said, 'Well, Mum and Dad are still in the wilds of South Australia with Aunt Hally, but they'd say get it cut up and the wood stored for winter. Get them to send the bill to me.'

'I can organise that.' It would give her something to do.

'OK, but if it gets too much for you come and stay. I can promise you an exciting life with a son who's discovered the joys of finger-painting and a daughter who has finally, thank the Lord, decided to sleep all night.'

'It sounds wonderful,' Ianthe said absently, for once not particularly interested in the progress of her goddaughter. 'I went into the water.'

She heard her friend's sudden intake of breath. 'How did it go?' Tricia asked eventually.

Briefly, keeping her voice even and emotionless, Ianthe gave her a concise account of the rescue.

'And do you think it's going to be all right?'

'Yes.' Ianthe looked out over the lake, shimmering blue beneath the tender sky. 'Yes,' she said slowly, 'I think it is.'

Tricia was delighted, and Ianthe hung up with a mirthless little smile. How ironic, she thought, that she should be saved from her phobia by this shattering grief, so intense that nothing else really seemed to matter.

Her father wasn't at home, but her stepmother said she'd tell him she was all right, and complained that her roses were covered in black spot after all the rain.

Ianthe made the right soothing noises, hanging up gratefully. She asked the store owner who'd be the right person to look at the macrocarpa tree, and rang the number.

'He's out,' his wife said. 'He's really busy after last night, but I'll take a message. What's your name?'

When Ianthe told her, she said, 'Oh, that's all right, your husband rang about the tree. A big macrocarpa, isn't it?'

'Yes,' Ianthe said hesitantly. 'My husband?' Alex, she thought, a tiny ember glowing warmly for a moment before collapsing into ashes.

'Yes, he rang a couple of hours ago, insisted that Doug look at it today. He'll be around before dark.'

'You were lucky,' Doug told her that evening, when Alex was leaving New Zealand. 'It was only a matter of time before it collapsed. OK, I'll be here tomorrow.'

While he and his son spent a hideous day reducing the tree to a pile of cut logs, the neighbours returned to mourn their battered marigolds. Ianthe handed over the key, and then, pummelled by the noise of the chainsaws, retreated to the shade of the pines by the motor camp—all still standing, she was relieved to see—and walked several times into the water, protected from panic by her fear for Alex.

In the blessed silence of evening she watched the television news. Nothing about Illyria. And nothing again in the morning. Sick with fear, Ianthe forced herself to fill the day with meaningless action, although she never remembered what she'd done. That evening, she again switched on the television, sitting jumpily through local and international news.

Still nothing. She was trying to persuade herself to cook some dinner, when the announcer said, 'And after a bloodless coup the long-lost prince of Illyria has returned and been crowned in an emotional ceremony.'

Ianthe froze as frenzied scenes flashed onto the screen, unable to see how such rioting could be bloodless. Alex, she thought, and that was when she gave up. The reporter's voice flowed on, and in the midst of the wild activity she could see him—Alex, the calm centre of the whirlwind, Alex whose face was set in lines of complete command, a man who had grown even further in mastery, who radiated a focused, formidable power.

He touched the eager hands held out to him, he spoke, he walked through that ecstatic, shrieking crowd alone, and by the sheer force of his will kept them from losing control and tipping into anarchy.

Wiping away the tears running down her cheeks, Ianthe forced herself to concentrate on the journalist.

'...towards the cathedral,' he was saying, 'where the archbishop is waiting to crown him. Rumours are flying—many of these people believe that the lost regalia has been found, and that the icon of Saint Ivan, the brother of the first prince of Illyria, now hangs in the cathedral. It was commonly believed that both regalia and icon—the most revered symbols of the princes of Illyria—had been destroyed at the time of the communist takeover.'

The images of cheering, rapturous Illyrians were replaced by that of a tree-lined plaza fronted by a cathedral, ancient, striped in green and white marble, packed with silent, kneeling people, their faces revealing awe and reverence and joy. Many were weeping.

And then there was the clangour of bells, and the kneeling people went mad.

'He had been in Illyria exactly three hours,' the reporter said, 'and single-handedly, by his mere presence, stopped the fighting. As soon as he was recognised—and in spite of his avowed intention to come only as a peacemaker—they rushed him to the cathedral and crowned him. Some of the ruling junta have been killed, but it is believed that most have escaped. The army and police force have come out solidly for the prince.'

The screen blurred, dissolved, and the newsreader's voice began on another item.

Ianthe got to her feet and switched off the set.

She'd told him how sorry she was for royalty, how intolerable she believed their life to be. Was that when he'd decided not to make love to her?

With an agonising, futile intensity, she wished she'd kept her mouth shut. Except that it wouldn't have made any difference. She hadn't changed her mind.

'The prince and the pauper,' she said aloud, her voice oddly detached. 'No, King Cophetua and the beggarmaid—and, in spite of the legend, I'll bet that didn't work out either.'

Any successful relationship needed more than desire. And although Alex had wanted her, he'd said nothing about love.

* * *

During the following days she wore herself out by wheeling the logs, barrow-load by barrow-load, into the back of the garage, where she stacked them carefully.

It was mindless work, and she functioned on automatic pilot, just as she ate and washed, just as she walked further into the lake each time. At night, exhausted by the effort, she slept heavily.

The long, tiring days were obscurely comforted by a small fantail. Two kilometres was too far for a bird that size to fly, so it couldn't possibly be the one she'd seen at Alex's house, but the tiny black bird with its high-pitched squeaks and round black eye and air of indomitable jauntiness did lift her spirits slightly.

Ianthe had believed she'd known grief. She had wept long for her laughing, daring Greg, enduring the savage pain and loneliness that had faded so reluctantly.

This was different. Perhaps because she had at least made love with Greg? Sometimes she wondered if she was going slightly mad. Torment, a wrenching, physical ache, an all-pervading shadow, blocked the light from her life. She dreamed of Alex, and woke with tears on her cheeks and a body racked with emptiness and anguish.

She refused to surrender to it. After all, nothing had happened—a few kisses, some long conversations, a violent, unappeased hunger.

Was this obsession? No! She wasn't ill. Merely, she thought one morning, lovesick...

It was time to pick up her life and go on with it, but first she had to fulfil her promise to Alex. Nightmares of teeth and blood, of death in the water, no longer woke her screaming from sleep, but as she walked across the sand a sly residue of sick panic clutched her stomach.

Setting her jaw, she waded out until she was one step from the boundary between milky water and the drop-off.

'Swim for me,' he'd said. 'Dive through that wall of blue...'

So she took in a deep breath and dived, down, down,

down, eyes open, into the heart of the blue. Once through the wall she hung motionless in the radiance of colour and hoped for the tide of life to warm her again.

Something broke inside her so that when she bobbed up to the surface she was crying, blinded by the sun and the water and the knowledge that although life would never be the same again, at least she'd taken the first step back to it.

CHAPTER EIGHT

'IANTHE, this is the opportunity of a lifetime.' Bill Fenn, famous for his wildlife documentaries, banged an exasperated fist down on the arm of his chair. 'The central lake in Illyria has never been scientifically examined—at least not by anyone with respectable academic credentials,' he qualified cunningly. 'And now we've got the go-ahead you can't just sit there po-faced as a koi carp and say you don't want to go!'

Ianthe's voice died in her throat. She swallowed and asked huskily, 'Did he contact you?'

'Who?'

The acrid taste of foolishness filled her mouth. Keeping her eyes on the small town of Russell that spread below her to the beach, she said reluctantly, 'The prince.'

'What prince? Oh, Alex Considine? No, why should he? He's too busy dragging his little realm into the modern world to bother about television programmes. We're merely a lowly documentary unit—very humble and unnecessary in his scheme of things. Even before he turned out to be the lost prince of Illyria he wouldn't have wiped his feet on us.'

Ianthe bit back a hot rebuttal; in spite of a recorded bloodline that stretched back over two thousand years Alex was no snob.

Bill's words smothered the small glimmer of hope that had lurked in her heart for the past year. To give herself time, she drained her coffee mug. 'Why me?' she demanded, thrusting out her leg. 'The scar's been tidied up, but it's still there.'

He didn't even look at it. 'You're the dolphin woman.

132

Not many people know more about dolphins than you do, and you're a hell of a lot better looking than anyone who does.'

Ianthe smiled ironically. 'That sounds like the Bill I know and love, but it's impossible. I've got excellent sponsorship for my research here, and I'm finally starting to see results. I don't want to go to Illyria.' There, she'd said the word. It reverberated through her brain, cold, clinking, painful. She picked herself up and plodded on, 'There must be someone else you could use. Shanna Pierce did a damned good job in my place.'

The producer frowned. 'She's studying green flatworms in the Coral Sea,' he said. 'Come on, Ianthe, you can get some grad student to take over here. We won't be away for more than a couple of months—four weeks if everything goes well. This is going to be really important; as far as we know not a single study has been done on those dolphins—not a scientific one, anyway. Doesn't it make your mouth water? We'll win another Wildscreen award with this; I can feel it in my bones.'

Shaking her head, Ianthe said lightly, 'Sorry. Why not just let the dolphins speak for themselves, with no human to interfere? I'd be happy to do the voice-over.'

He leaned back and stared out across the little town, over the waters of the upper harbour and at the bush-covered hills beyond, many starred with houses.

Frowning, he said, 'Because you've got this affinity with them, that's why. They come when you call.' Ignoring her splutter of disbelieving amusement, he went on, 'Damn it, Ianthe, why are you being so bloody-minded? We've been trying to get permission to go to Illyria since before the communists were kicked out, but they wouldn't let us near the place, and neither would the lot that took over after them. Now we've finally got the go-ahead and you won't budge! Did the shark eat your common sense too? Illyria is new ground.'

'New water, actually,' Ianthe murmured.

He grinned and visibly relaxed. 'And what water! A lake fifty miles long and twenty wide, complete with freshwater dolphins, trapped in there for twelve million years. Hell, no one even knows how many there are.'

Oh, Bill knew her well. Ianthe wanted to see those dolphins so much she could taste the desire on her tongue. But she couldn't go; Alex had almost certainly given permission for the unit to film in Illyria convinced she was no longer connected to it. If she turned up he might well think she was chasing him. The very thought shrivelled her backbone.

'There are other scientists—'

Bill fixed her with a sharp, intense stare. 'We won those awards—four of them, Ianthe, one the green Oscar!—with you, and you were featured in each citation. The judges loved the way you combined serious professional and scientific enthusiasm with a knack for popularising science. It helped that the camera adores your pretty face, but that's not everything and you know it.'

She waved towards the smooth waters of the innermost Bay of Islands. 'Bill, I've got enough work here to keep me busy for years. I like it here—the people are lovely and the dolphins are particularly co-operative.'

His dark gaze glittered. 'Look, this is a chance to show that our Wildscreen award wasn't just a fluke. New Zealand's already got a brilliant reputation in the wildlife area, but if we pull this off we can head for the stars.'

Getting to her feet, Ianthe walked across to the railing. Another operation had cleaned up the scar and reduced the limp, so although she'd never walk straight again her uneven gait was nowhere near so obvious as it had been.

Anyway, a limp didn't matter in the water. And now, thanks to the black misery that had overwhelmed her after Alex's departure, the water held no terrors.

When, a short time after she'd watched the wild outpouring of emotion and hope that had been Alex's coronation, she'd been contacted by a firm who'd offered sponsorship for her work in the Bay of Islands, she'd accepted without hesitation. In a way the sponsorship had saved her. Work had provided the impetus to force her through her private hell and win the struggle for some sort of peace.

And now, twelve months later, Bill had shattered that difficult serenity.

'I really don't—'

'Ianthe, don't turn it down straight away. Think about it overnight.'

He thought she was mad to refuse, and in a way she was. Perhaps she should treat it as some sort of exorcism.

Turning from the bright view of the Bay, she said, 'All right, I'll think about it.'

'Let me know tomorrow.' He gave her an ironic smile. 'And forget what I said before. Nobody's indispensable.'

Her smile matched his. 'I know.'

'But it would be a pity to miss out—it would help keep the sponsorship dollars rolling in. Who's doing it?'

She told him.

'A good catch,' he said casually. 'They'd really like it if you gave that husky laugh a few more times on the little screen. And don't cut your hair!'

Self-consciously Ianthe pushed a long strand over her shoulder. 'I haven't agreed yet.'

After waving Bill goodbye she walked into the house she'd rented for the year. A small, elderly cottage, it wasn't exactly comfortable, but it was cheap, so the sponsorship money had been stretched to include a fax and a computer—one that ran on Alex's software.

Blinking, she remembered an ancient ceremony lit by flaring candles...

Such a modern man, and yet Alex had been completely at home in that huge cathedral, watched over by old icons hastily dragged out from wherever the clergy had hidden them. Beneath an antique crown his pale eyes had burned like flames, and the dark, dynamic features had promised strength and fortitude and courage.

During the past year she'd tried to ignore Illyria. It hadn't been too hard—once the romantic, astonishing return of the prince had become old news there'd been little in the media—but she knew that he'd begun reforms, although not without first setting up a system of consultation and communication with the people of his small state.

She was over him now. Whatever she'd felt had been a holiday passion, all the more potent and memorable because it had been frustrated.

Alex, she thought now with a wry, heartbreaking twist to her smile, had come to the lakes to make a decision, and he'd known that in his new life there would be no room for her. And, because of that over-developed sense of responsibility, he'd rejected her even though she'd made it obvious she wanted him.

One day she'd probably be grateful for that.

Perhaps she needed a final goodbye, some symbolic farewell that would force her longing heart to accept an ending and release her from the power his memory still wielded. Alex's destiny had been made for him before he was born, and except for those few days last summer, when their lives had briefly touched, they had widely separated futures.

Her forefinger traced lightly around the keyboard. It was ridiculous to think of the software she relied on every day as a connection, yet she did.

Should she go to Illyria?

Not if there was any chance of meeting him again, but Alex was too busy ruling his country to bother about itinerant film-makers.

And it would, she thought, provide that closure. She mightn't see him, but she'd see the country that had bred him, the people whose blood ran in his veins, the culture that had given him strength. A trip to Illyria would hurt, but it would be a clean pain, one that might finally heal the misery that still ached through her.

Yes, she'd go.

*   *   *

Just before midnight six weeks later she stood awkwardly beside her suitcase in an arrivals hall half a world away, looking around for a familiar face. The press of people—some still waiting, some locked in fervent embraces—the tears, the laughter, the loud voices in a language that sounded a little like Italian, exhausted her. Blinking, she gazed around. Most people ignored her, but from the response of those who noticed her she deduced that blonde hair was rare in Illyria; she probably stood out like a haystack in a coal yard.

No team member surged through the crowd; no stranger held up a piece of cardboard with her name on it. Feeling like an unwanted guest at a party, she waited with her bags at her feet until almost everyone had collected their visitors and the chatter had died away.

Oh, wonderful, she thought, with the bleakness that travelling from the opposite side of the world engendered. Stranded...

Pull yourself together, she told herself stringently. The team was staying in a guesthouse in the city. Rummaging in her bag, she found her address book and turned to the page where she'd copied down the name. She'd get a taxi. No problems.

Outside she hesitated, peering through the soft night for the taxi rank. Before she had time to note that it was empty, a uniformed man got out of a limousine—gangster-black and lengthy—and came forward, snatching her case from her with an exclamation of horror.

'It's all right, thank you,' she said.

Clearly he didn't understand English—well, why should he?—but he smiled at her, stowed her luggage into the boot and ushered her into the back seat.

It smelt of cigarettes. Wrinkling her nose, she settled back. Soon—very soon—she'd have that shower she craved, and then fall into bed and sleep for at least twelve hours.

They travelled through the dark countryside for about

twenty minutes before entering the city. Ianthe gazed out of the shaded windows at sparsely lighted streets in which a harmonious mixture of buildings from many periods was marred by some square, ungracious concrete monstrosities. The narrow streets wound higher and higher, finally ending in a huge wall, with an archway through which they drove past guards.

Stunned, Ianthe realised that the guesthouse was part of a castle, though they were crossing the forecourt and turning, thank heavens, a corner, away from the ceremonial entrance with its two rifle-carrying sentries.

As the car drew to a halt, close to a suitably inconspicuous door guarded by only one sentry, Ianthe sat up, rigid with shock.

This wasn't *a* castle; this was *the* castle.

Alex is here, she thought, the secret, unbidden excitement that had purred away inside her since she'd known she was coming to Illyria beginning to stretch, to glow, to fill her with a rich, wild delight.

Later she decided she must have been suffering from terminal jet lag. She'd got into the car without being addressed by name, and now she went docilely into the castle with the slim, slender man of middle age who came out to greet her with a brisk, professional courtesy.

'This way, madam,' he said, ushering her up the steps.

Ianthe walked beside him automatically, along a wide hall furnished with dark green carpet and suits of armour shining against the stone walls like props from some Hollywood epic. To her astonishment they got into a lift.

Weird, she thought, her brain clogged with exhaustion. Alice-in-Wonderland stuff.

After a slow, dignified ascent the lift eased to a stop. Another corridor greeted them, this time carpeted in blue, and with white panelling. Clearly some previous prince, disliking the rough strength of the original castle walls, had redecorated. No suits of armour here; the walls were hung

with ancestors. All of them seemed to have Alex's
eyes—startlingly pale in the hawk-featured faces.

Whoever's genes they were, Ianthe thought, they were
damned prepotent.

'Madam,' the man with her said.

He'd stopped and was holding open a door. Gratefully,
Ianthe walked past, saying, 'Thank you.'

The door closed behind him and she was standing alone,
staring stupidly around at the elegant, elaborate furniture of
an eighteenth-century drawing room.

Ianthe shivered and rubbed her arms. Her brain had
turned to cotton wool and she couldn't think.

She wandered over to the windows, surprised that they
were proper panes and not thin arrow slits. Leaning forward, she peered out across the city. Over there were mountains, and the lake—or perhaps she was looking down on
the harbour.

While the world's fickle attention had been caught by the
drama of Alex's return, commentators had spent much
news time on political analysis, pontificating on whether
any man could coax a tiny, poverty-stricken principality
into the twenty-first century.

They'd missed the point, Ianthe thought now. You didn't
turn a one-man operation into a hugely successful company
without being ruthless and disciplined—and without having
an excellent understanding of humankind. If anyone could
do it successfully, Alex could.

Yawning, she turned away from the window.

Her heart jumped into her throat, because walking
through the door was Alex. He faltered in midstep, translucent eyes glacial, his beautiful mouth hardening into a
thin line, then came into the room.

'What the hell are you doing here?' he demanded.

Hope shattered. She said huskily, 'I—somebody picked
me up at the airport. I'm here to make a documentary about
dolphins. With Bill Fenn. I thought you knew about it.'

'I knew.' The pale gaze flicked across her face.

Clearly he hadn't known she was part of the team. Ianthe could have cringed. She knew exactly what she looked like—crumpled and tired, her usual vigour dimmed by over thirty hours of flying.

Straightening her shoulders, she tried for a crisp tone. 'Well, I'm working with the unit again. Where are they?'

'At the guesthouse. Obviously there's been a mix-up, but don't worry—you can spend the night here.'

'No, I'd… That is, it can't be very far.'

'They won't be expecting you now. It's late and you're exhausted,' Alex said curtly, pulling a long bell cord.

Almost as though he'd been waiting for the summons, a man arrived, youngish, dark. Alex spoke to him and the servant bowed. In English Alex said, 'He'll take you to a room and provide you with a maid.'

'I don't need a maid,' she said quickly.

The cold eyes narrowed. 'You do,' he said with exquisite courtesy. 'I'm sorry for the confusion. I hope you sleep well tonight. Tomorrow morning, when you're ready, you'll be taken to the guesthouse.'

Ianthe nodded. 'All right,' she said. His detachment flayed her emotions, revealing her precious serenity for what it was—a fool's delusion. 'Goodnight,' she said, stumbling over the word.

His gaze didn't soften. 'Goodnight.'

Obediently she followed the servant out of the room. They walked up a set of stairs and along another over-decorated hall, and then the man showed her into a room, bowed, and backed out. Ianthe looked around the huge room, noting the four-poster set on its dais, the desk and sofa and blanket chest, the wall hangings. Her head throbbed and unspoken emotions blocked her throat.

Almost immediately a woman bustled in, middle-aged, sharp-faced, her black hair drawn into a neat bun. After a smile and a greeting in what was presumably Illyrian, she opened the door to a man who brought in Ianthe's suitcase and hand luggage. When he'd left, she gestured towards the locks. Ianthe opened the case, and within minutes found herself in a bath in the next room, gratefully scrubbing herself down with soap that smelt of herbs and listening to the woman hum as she unpacked.

It was such a comfortable sound that it thawed a small corner of Ianthe's frozen heart. Eventually she got out and dried herself, draped a bath sheet above her breasts, and walked into the bedroom to find a nightgown laid out on the bed and the woman gathering up an armful of clothes. When she saw Ianthe she smiled, said something, and imitated the movements of an iron.

Too weary and heartsick to try communicating, Ianthe smiled and nodded, then obeyed the woman's gesture and got into the bed.

It could have been a bed of thorns; she wouldn't have known. Sleep—draining, voracious—claimed her and she surrendered eagerly to its dark embrace.

Some time later she woke abruptly, as though shocked out of unconsciousness. Unreasoning terror gripped her, driving her from the bed across to the window. Twitching back a curtain, she looked down into the dimly lit forecourt. As she watched, a man strode out of the building.

Alex, she thought, her heart contracting. He got into the car, which left the courtyard and wound its way down into the shadowed city.

An enormous, depthless sadness clutched her heart. She hugged her arms around herself and rocked back and forth, soundlessly crying her grief into the alien sky.

At length she turned away, aching with the pressure of the unshed tears that burned behind her eyes. Tomorrow she'd be out of here, welcomed into the familiar, safe camaraderie of the team.

Yet while she'd been with Alex that safety and familiarity had meant nothing. For a moment—until she realised that he'd been appalled to see her—she'd almost believed that if Alex had loved her she'd gladly leave her world and make herself a part of his.

But he couldn't even bear to stay in the castle with her!

Ianthe limped across the room, climbed back into the bed, and courted the dreamless bliss of unconsciousness. She managed it in snatches, but she was awake more than she was asleep, listening to the sounds of an unknown place, learning the true meaning of loneliness.

Alex had a destiny to follow and so did she. Right from the moment they'd met he'd made it clear that they had no possibility of a linked future. Perhaps, if he hadn't been the lost prince—but, no, it was impossible. *She* was impossible. She wouldn't have fitted into the world of a very rich man—the fact that he now ruled this small country merely reinforced her unsuitability. She'd wither and die in the rarefied atmosphere of a court, however modern.

Even if—oh, faint chance—even if there'd been any sort of relationship between them she wouldn't have followed him to Illyria. The thought filled her with horror. It would mean giving up the career she found so fascinating, it would mean she had no freedom—no, she couldn't bear it.

This was familiar ground. Each tired, truthful argument had rattled around in her head for months until she'd firmly banished them and got on with her life. Alex might have wanted to make love with her, but he was an honourable man, and honourable men didn't make love to unsuitable women when they were planning to claim a throne that had been in their family for over a thousand years.

For the first time Ianthe admitted that what she'd felt after he left was grief for something that had never existed. It made her seem so stupid—like some poor woman afflicted with erotomania, whose madness was such that she could turn a definite rejection into a seductive signal. She couldn't allow herself to hope that he'd somehow organised this jaunt so that he could see her again, because that way lay the tormented, dangerous path of obsession.

And if he had he'd have written to her, instead of ignoring her existence this past year.

Of course she woke late, feeling more tired than when

she'd gone to sleep, and was greeted by the maid carrying a tray; with her was another woman, also middle-aged, elegant and slim, dressed by a couturier. Completely at sea, Ianthe sat bolt-upright.

'Hello,' this woman said, smiling, although her dark eyes were disconcertingly direct and cool. 'I'm Serena Considine—Alex's mother, you know—and you are Ianthe Brown. Alex asked me to come because I speak English. Welcome to Illyria. Leola has breakfast for you, and after you've eaten it and got up I'll take you to your film team, who are just outside the castle walls in the guesthouse.'

Ianthe asked slowly, 'How on earth did I get here?'

Smiling, Alex's mother said lightly, 'Oh, a silly mistake! Don't worry about it. Unfortunately the prince isn't able to be here this morning, but he asked me to say that he was delighted to give you hospitality and that he hopes you have had a pleasant and refreshing night.'

Ianthe's smile was as artificial as Alex's good wishes. Although husky with sleep, her voice didn't tremble when she replied, 'Thank you. I won't be long.'

The woman nodded and smiled again, this time with a little more warmth, and watched while Leola carefully put the tray over Ianthe's knees.

'If there's anything you need,' Serena Considine said, 'ring for Leola. The time now is nine o'clock, so I'll be waiting at ten-thirty to take you to the guesthouse.'

'Thank you.' Ianthe hoped that her expression didn't give away her desolation.

After the two women left she looked at the food—a warm roll and jam, slices of melon and peach—and a silver pot of delicious-smelling coffee. The thought of eating made her stomach lurch, but starving herself would be stupid. Clearly she wasn't going to see Alex again, so she might just as well get out of the castle, do the job she came here for, and then she could go home and forget him.

When she arrived back in New Zealand would be soon enough to wish that she and Alex had never met. Except that, she thought, breaking the roll open, she couldn't bear the thought of not having known him.

It just didn't seem fair that somehow her wayward heart had learned to love him even though she'd known it was hopeless. The roll tasted like ashes, but she forced herself to chew, to swallow, to drink the flavourless coffee. If she dwelt on the years that stretched with grey endlessness in front of her she'd go mad, so she'd just grit her teeth and take each day as it came.

It was only in Victorian novels that women suffered all their lives from unrequited love and died still faithful to a memory. Love like that—the sort that lasted for eternity—was an illusion.

An unhealthy illusion, she told herself sternly.

The team greeted her with affection and much teasing about what they insisted was her bid for royal status.

'I thought you were going to meet me,' she protested as they escorted her into a small meeting room with a large table.

Someone poured her a cup of coffee and pushed it in front of her as she sat down.

Bill said, 'We would have, if you'd been on the flight you said you were going to be on. It comes in tonight.'

'That was the original plan; then a plane got grounded somewhere and they couldn't get me a connection from London today so I had to come a day earlier. But I sent you a fax telling you of the change.'

'It didn't get here,' Bill said cheerfully. 'Not to worry, sweetie, we know how efficient you are so we'll accept that you sent it. And it got you a night in the prince's bed! Not many people can claim that.'

She hid the jerk of sensation in her stomach by asking, 'So when do we leave for the camp?'

'We don't have a camp this time. It's the lap of luxury for us—a fishing lodge right on the lake shore, with servants and everything a prince can lay on laid on. We go early tomorrow morning, even if the reception keeps us up late.'

'What reception?'

He lifted his brows at the sharp query. 'The prince's reception,' he said tolerantly. 'Tonight. Best bib and tucker. But before that we're having a meeting to finalise details, and then we're separating to do our various things. You have an appointment at the museum.'

'Great.' Panic gripped her; taking a deep breath she tried to muster the enthusiasm he clearly expected.

Bill grinned. 'Our contact says they've found a pod of dolphins, and they're eagerly looking forward to the filming.'

Still thrown by the mention of a reception, Ianthe asked stupidly, 'The pod?'

Everyone around the table laughed. 'Yeah,' the cameraman teased, 'they sent a special message to say so.'

'What sort of reception?' she asked doggedly, adding, 'I want to know which clothes to wear.'

Bill looked impatient. 'Oh, the usual thing. The prince says that a formal reception will make it obvious that he's all in favour. You always manage to look good whatever you wear, so you'll be fine. Just bat your lashes and flick a curl or two. The locals love blondes.'

Ianthe needed the quick caffeine charge of coffee, yet she didn't dare lift her cup in case she spilt it. 'It makes sense, I suppose,' she said distantly, 'although I didn't realise anyone would be suspicious about us.'

'Well, there's some legend connected with the dolphins. They're emblems of the ruling house, and the locals are a bit touchy about them.'

He nodded at a plaster crest over the doorway, its colours and gilding patently new. Blue waves supported three gold dolphins, one blowing some sort of trumpet, one armed with a spear, and the third carrying a mermaid.

'We have to convince everyone that we don't intend to harm them,' he said. 'It's the one tiny fly in the ointment, but I'm glad it's there—otherwise it would all be far too easy. You know, everything has fallen into place so smoothly it should worry the hell out of me, but I've got a good, good feeling about this. It was meant. We're going to make magic in Illyria.'

I'm glad for you, Ianthe thought, all her rationalisations stripped away to reveal the truth.

If this wasn't love, she thought feverishly, at last managing to get her cup to her lips under cover of the conversation, it might just as well be, because the thought of seeing Alex again at once thrilled her unbearably and tossed her deep into the pits of despair.

She had all day to mend her defences. She could do it—meet him again and smile—because nothing had happened. They had met not as a millionaire prince and a marine biologist-cum-television presenter; they'd been two people who'd found each other interesting and attractive.

That was all.

'Hey, don't go to sleep on us now!' Bill commanded, breaking into her thoughts. 'You've got work to do. Our courier has organised the local museum into assembling all the literature about the dolphins they can find. You'll have an interpreter to translate, but it'll be a long day. Do you want some more coffee?'

'No, thanks. I've studied the scientific literature—such as it is,' she said.

'Of course you have. This is more cultural and traditional. A lot of these books were smuggled away or hidden when the communists took over.'

Like the icon and the crown, she thought, remembering that strange, passionate ceremony in the cathedral.

'Everyone's being very helpful,' she said slowly.

'Yeah. Makes a nice change to some places we've been. Remember the time we went to that island in the Marquesas, not realising it was taboo for a woman to set foot on it?'

'I remember,' she said feelingly. 'One of the more terrifying moments of my life.'

'Well, you kept your head. At least you didn't really set foot on it, as we pointed out, and you were suitably contrite. They took one look at your big golden eyes and worried little face and forgave you.'

'I don't know that they forgave me,' she said, uncomfortable as she always was when someone referred to her looks. 'They knew I hadn't intended to cause any harm. And,' she added with a note of cynicism, 'they weren't so out of touch with the world that they didn't know you can't murder people without getting unpleasant feedback. If they'd killed me they'd have had to kill us all, and quite frankly I don't think they had the stomach for it.'

'You know,' Bill teased, 'you're just not romantic, that's your problem. Ah, well, off to work, boys and girl. It's going to be a busy day.'

CHAPTER NINE

HE WAS right; she spent the day with people who were so eager to help they exhausted her. Fascinated by the many intimate, intricate ways the dolphins of Illyria were wound into the people's art and legends, Ianthe would normally have enjoyed every moment of it.

It was, however, hard to concentrate with an axe suspended above her head.

As the car climbed from the museum back to the guest-house she allowed herself the forbidden luxury of a question or two about life in Illyria under the previous regime. Graciela, the interpreter—a thin woman in her early thirties who'd been pointing out the important buildings in the town—answered with unforced eagerness.

'Oh, it is so different now! Before was—grey, with our lives so regulated and circumscribed, and then when communism collapsed there were three terrible years. But now our prince has come back and our world is revolving the way it is supposed to.'

'He must find it strange to rule a country he knows so little about,' Ianthe said.

Graciela shook her head vigorously. 'He lived here until he was ten years, you know. They are the important years, those ones of childhood. He and his parents worked in the fields with the peasants, so he knows us very well!'

Startled, Ianthe asked, 'Why did they do that? Were they being punished by the new rulers?'

'Oh, no! *They* didn't know the prince and his wife were still in Illyria. Prince Ivan chose to stay with us rather than flee; he set up an underground movement—many opponents of the regime were guided through the mountains to

Italy by the prince or the people who helped him. So of course the people loved him and protected him and his wife, and his son when he was born.'

After digesting this Ianthe said slowly, 'He must have been a brave man.'

'Our princes are always brave! But when Prince Alexi was aged ten years someone betrayed them. His father gave his life to save his wife and his son; they went over the mountains in the depths of winter, and made their way secretly to Australia. Everyone thought they were Italian, I think. They lived in a small town in Australia until he went to university. Then he became a computer expert and made much money, which he is now using to help us. But he always knew who he was.'

And, rather than see his people massacred in their silent protest by a corrupt and vengeful regime, or turn on each other in civil warfare, he'd accepted a life he must be finding restrictive.

'I saw the coronation on television,' Ianthe said, looking at the striped cathedral, exotically Romanesque beside its tall Venetian belltower. 'Why was he snatched from the airport and brought here and crowned so quickly?'

'We thought he might leave us,' the interpreter told her frankly. 'He said he came back as a peacemaker, not a prince. We wanted peace, but we knew that it would only come with our prince, so we crowned him straight away. Then he couldn't go.'

So he'd meant it, that afternoon at the lakes, when he'd said he didn't want to rule. She said, 'It seems to have worked. Everything looks very peaceful now.'

'It is the only thing that could have worked,' Graciela told her firmly. 'He has reconciled us with each other; we are a united people. Oh, there are scars—some of us will never forget that many people helped those who ruled us so cruelly—but he has made us see that revenge only creates the need for more revenge. Also, because he is a very good businessman, he knows how to rule people, and because he is our prince the people trust him. And,' she finished with a laugh, 'because he is so handsome we are all in love with him. Although it is time for him to marry, we want him to be happy, so we look at the candidates with a suspicious eye. Only the best is good enough for our prince.'

Distantly Ianthe asked, 'How many candidates are there?'

'There is a very lovely young aristocrat from England who would do well, and also a chic Frenchwoman. But you understand there have been rumours of others—a film star or two, a singer.'

Ianthe's smile was wooden. 'I suppose any possible wife has to be aristocratic.'

The interpreter shrugged. 'It would probably be better, because they are accustomed to the life, but me, I don't care. I just hope that he will be happy and have children and stay with us.' The car swung into the gravel forecourt of the guesthouse. She turned and said, 'I must tell you how interesting I have found this day and wish you every good luck for your film. When will it be ready for us to see?'

Ianthe said, 'Not for at least a year, I'm afraid.' When it showed on Illyrian television she'd be back in New Zealand with a handful of memories—pathetic little souvenirs of an unrequited love.

Before she got maudlin she began to thank Graciela.

'It is nothing,' the interpreter said with a quick gesture. 'I enjoyed the day. Now, you have your phrases correct? Say them to me.'

Earlier in the day Ianthe had asked her for the most common and useful phrases—a greeting, please, thank you, goodbye, you are so kind...

Graciela had written them down and Ianthe had practised them at odd intervals. She repeated them now, frowning slightly in her effort to get both words and accent correct.

'Excellent!' the interpreter said warmly. 'Illyrian is not

too difficult to learn for it is a Romance language, you understand. The Romans were here for hundreds of years—they defeated the Illyrians—and then there were wars and battles until a thousand years later there was just this little principality. But we have had clever princes, ruthless and battle-hardy and brave—all with those pale, pale eyes that came from a Saxon princess many many centuries ago—and they have kept us separate and ourselves. We look to the future with another clever, courageous, ruthless prince.'

'Ruthless?' Ianthe objected.

'Oh, I think so, do you not?' The interpreter nodded briskly. 'To build such a big corporation a man must be more than a little ruthless, and to run a country he must be ruthless too. There are hard decisions to be made; he must temper his natural mercy with what will be best for the country. Yes, I think ruthlessness will be useful.'

By then the chauffeur had opened the door. As Ianthe got out she said in Illyrian, 'Thank you, and may God bless you and your children.'

'Very good!' Graciela clapped her hands as the car drew away.

Ianthe turned and saw that the porter who had come down to meet her was smiling too. She said, 'Thank you,' in careful Illyrian, and went into the guesthouse to get ready for the reception.

Hours later she looked in the mirror. A young maid had arrived to ask her if she wanted help; although Ianthe had refused the woman had stayed, inconspicuously tidying the room. Strangely, Ianthe didn't feel self-conscious as she carefully blow-dried her hair and put on make-up.

When she got out her honey-coloured bodysuit the maid vanished into the bathroom, not emerging until Ianthe had donned a silk skirt and shirt in soft shades of tawny gold and bronze and muted rust.

Insensibly cheered, Ianthe returned the woman's appreciative smile. She was so jittery her nerves thrummed like wires in the wind; in ten minutes she'd be seeing Alex again.

Ianthe touched perfume—her favourite, Ricci's Les Belles—to her wrists and beneath her ears. She slipped into a pair of bronze shoes with low heels—wishing foolishly that she could still wear high heels, wishing that she didn't limp—and picked up a bag in a slightly darker colour.

Beaming, the maid said something, then added, 'Chic.'

'Thank you,' Ianthe responded in Illyrian.

The woman's face lit up and she said something else in the same language, laughing a little when Ianthe shook her head and said, 'No, I'm sorry, that's almost all I know.'

Still smiling, the woman nodded and held the door open.

No doubt the servants went with the guesthouse. In spite of the luxurious surroundings this was probably where visitors of less importance were put up. Real notables presumably stayed at the castle.

So just who had she been mistaken for the previous night? The French aristocrat or the British one?

Ianthe's stomach contracted. Straight-backed, her heart thudding unevenly, she walked down the stairs and into the foyer where the rest of the crew were waiting. Accustomed to wearing shorts and T-shirts most of the time, they looked vaguely uneasy in suits.

One gave a low wolf-whistle as she walked towards them, and Bill commented, 'You know, it's totally unfair that women should be able to pack their good clothes into the equivalent of a paper bag.'

'We need some advantages,' she said, trying to sound her normal amiable self.

'OK, guys, let's go,' he said. 'The car's outside.'

Ianthe protested, 'But the castle's only next door.'

'I gather it isn't done to walk. Etiquette, you know.'

So they drove under the archway, and the guards stared straight ahead as the car stopped before the ceremonial entrance.

Inside, she noticed the smell—not musty, not unpleasant, but old. In New Zealand any building more than a hundred years old was treasured. These stone walls and the flag-stoned floor spoke of centuries.

As the lift wheezed slowly upwards she stared straight ahead, unable to concentrate on the banter around her. It wasn't surprising that Alex, who'd been completely at home in the spare, modern elegance of the house by the lake, should be equally so in this ancient fortress. His in-born self-assurance would see him through any situation, any setting.

Pride held her head high, although dread and anticipation had built to such a fever pitch that she'd shut down into numbness. Walking steadily beside Bill, she followed the uniformed servant through a door and into a salon. She got a confused impression of colour—a rich, deep crimson, much oyster white and some gold flourishes—and French furniture, with more portraits on the wall interspersed with large landscapes.

Alex came forward to meet them, introducing himself with pleasant informality. Although he smiled, the arctic eyes were unreadable.

'Welcome to the palace again,' he said, shaking her hand as though they were total strangers. 'I'm sorry I wasn't here to greet you this morning, but I hope you had a pleasant night and that the arrangements worked this time.'

'They did, thank you, sir,' she said, stepping back as Bill introduced the rest of the crew.

And that was that.

She'd thought that meeting Alex would be the worst thing, but she'd been wrong, for Alex's mother was es-corting a fair-haired woman who—inevitably—turned out to be the daughter of an English duke. This, Ianthe realised immediately, was the woman the limousine driver had mis-taken her for.

Lady Sophie was beautiful in a cool English way, and she possessed a cool English charm. Apparently she also had royal connections, whatever that meant. Ianthe would have felt much better if she'd been able to dislike the woman, but it was impossible.

Jealousy, she discovered, was both acid and undignified.

So she concentrated on her behaviour. She smiled a lot and told people what she did with the film unit, and while the room filled up she glanced around and saw the team busy making friends. It was part of the job; you never knew when someone could smooth the way for the unit. Besides, it created a little stir of interest, and that was good too.

According to Bill, as the only woman in the unit she provided the glamour, and until that moment she'd never believed that the chatting and the smiles and some very mild flirtation compromised her integrity.

But now she watched Bill smile deeply into a middle-aged woman's eyes and felt cheap, second-rate, slightly grubby.

Still, she thought cynically, that was better than the raw resentment that burned through her when she thought of Alex with another woman. Beneath the jealousy lurked a darker, more primitive pain, the anguish of loss and bereavement, a sense of betrayal and incompletion as though something had been torn from her.

So stupid. All stemming from her first glance at Alex just over a year ago; it had altered her at some deep, cellular level, and she was beginning to suspect that she'd never be able to change back again.

'Have you settled in yet?'

Even the sound of his voice resonated through her with the force and power of a master playing an instrument. 'Yes, thank you, sir,' she said, turning slowly so that she could regain control of her features, of her eyes. Her heart sped up, and the forbidden pleasure of being in the same room with him sent adrenalin washing through her.

Alex was studying her with eyes like chips of blue ice, his lean, autocratic features and the mouth that could send her to paradise ruthlessly controlled. 'Cut out the sir,' he said evenly.

'I thought it was protocol.'

'You were being provocative.' His eyes gleamed and the beginnings of a smile—taut, intimidating—touched the corners of his mouth.

She shrugged. 'Sorry.'

His lashes drooped, half hiding a gaze both molten and cutting as the flame in the heart of a diamond. He drawled, 'Don't be sorry. I admire your spirit, but this is neither the time nor the place.' And before she had a chance to take this in, he continued, 'I'm sorry for the mix-up last night.'

She could smile. It hurt, and the curve of her lips was meaningless, but she could do it. She said lightly, 'Oh, I realise that your driver must have mistaken me for Lady Sophie. I hope she didn't arrive to find nobody waiting.'

'She'd have managed,' he said, that penetrating gaze unwavering. 'Her message to say she wasn't coming until this morning didn't get through.'

'So all's well...'

He gave her a sardonic smile. 'I hope so.'

Driven by some imp of perversity, Ianthe said, 'I'm sorry my presence drove you out of the castle last night. You didn't really need to go, you know. Or to let me stay, since the guesthouse is just outside the walls.'

'You looked as though you were going to drop in your shoes,' he said coolly. 'It was simpler to let you stay here. As for leaving—it was necessary. If word had got around that you and I had spent the night in the castle—and it would have, believe me—everyone would have assumed that you are my mistress.'

Colour bit hard on her skin. And what, she wanted to ask, about the lovely Lady Sophie. Where did she stay? Or did the fact that she was aristocratic, a candidate for marriage, automatically put a stop to such rumours?

With an edge of shrillness Ianthe said, 'So it is like living in a goldfish bowl?'

'Yes,' he said silkily, 'just as you said.'

'How can you bear it?'

He shrugged, his face aloof and unreadable. 'Most of it is the kind of natural curiosity you have about relatives and close friends. Because the Illyrians have had to fight for their independence down the years, they tend to think of themselves as a huge family—one that includes my mother and me.' He paused, then said deliberately, 'When I decided to come back I didn't realise that their first move would be to hijack me and crown me.'

Amazed, she responded swiftly, 'I know.'

'I really did think I could fly in, make peace, and then fly back to my own world. Even so, the decision to return was bloody difficult. I had a very pleasant life—' his smile was a masterpiece of ironic detachment '—and coming to Illyria was the last thing I wanted to do. Especially as I couldn't tell you what I was trying to work out.'

'I must have been a damned nuisance.'

His mouth straightened as he looked above her. 'Not at all,' he said with remote courtesy.

Ianthe turned her head slightly and saw that he was watching the charming, lovely Lady Sophie. Brutal anger almost snapped through the guard she'd set on her tongue, but she reined it in. 'I won't keep you from your duties,' she said. 'Thank you for making it so easy for us to film—we're all very grateful. And we hope that the result will do justice to Illyria and its treasures.'

Mockery gleamed in the arctic eyes. 'Oh, I'm sure it will,' he said. 'Your limp is much less obvious; I presume the scar is gone also?'

'No,' she said flatly. 'It will always be there, but Bill doesn't seem to think it matters.'

'Of course it doesn't.' His gaze lingered on her face, then flicked for a long, deliberate moment to her mouth. When he began to speak again it was with an intensity that was all the more potent for being leashed by will-power. 'As well as being intelligent, with a rare ability to make complex ideas easily understood, you're lovely enough to ravish any camera lens. Apart from having your leg operated on, what have you been doing this last year?'

Dry-mouthed, acutely responsive to the smouldering undercurrent in his voice and gaze, she looked desperately away. What the hell was he doing, flirting with her in front of the woman who was quite possibly going to be his wife?

Good manners held her captive. It would be appallingly rude to swing on her heel and leave him. And, of course, if she offended him he might rescind their opportunity to film the dolphins.

Which was mean-spirited and nasty of her—he wouldn't stoop to such measures. Dredging up what little composure she could find, she gave him an aloof look and said, 'I've got over my fear of the water.'

'I assumed that, as you have your job back.'

'Oh, no, this is only a temporary job, a one-off. I've gone back to the Bay of Islands. Soon after you left I got offered enough sponsorship to keep my research going for three years if I'm careful.'

The dark brows met for a second. 'Indeed,' he said blandly. 'Three years. So what exactly are you trying to find out about the dolphins there?'

'I'm particularly interested in which dolphin is related to which, and how they work as a community.' Her reply was stiff, but with more questions she relaxed, although she was still acutely aware of the change in him. The previous night he'd looked at her with a cold, almost antagonistic attitude; now he had—not exactly softened, but he'd become more as he'd been a year ago: magnetic in an incisive male way, interested in her and her thoughts and her work.

Yet the effects from that moment of sensual anticipation, when he'd looked at her mouth and his eyes had flamed, still shivered across her nerve-ends. She'd made love with Greg, she'd kissed Alex and wanted him ferociously, but that tiny, primally sexual caress was the most erotic thing that had ever happened to her, and its effects sang relent-lessly through her body in a slow tide of heat.

Coming to Illyria had been the biggest mistake in her life. She should have refused; seeing Alex again had fanned her emotions into fierce life, and this time, she suspected, she wouldn't be able to smother them into silence.

Every tiny alteration in his deep voice reverberated through her, sharpening her senses. She reacted acutely to the charm that smoothed over the dark authority in his tone, to the way various words enchanted her ear, betraying those years spent as a child in Illyria, to the clean, austere beauty of his features, to the powerful sexual impact that enmeshed her in a primeval sorcery as old as man and woman.

For a moment he'd revealed an untamed masculine de-sire, swiftly smothered but bold and reckless. And even as excitement burned through her inhibitions she knew it wasn't enough. She needed more than Alex's desire, more than the passionate fulfilment of sex with him.

She wanted his love. Panic kicked in her stomach. Oh, God, she thought desperately, what am I going to do now?

She'd been staring at the knot of his tie. Unable to help herself, she looked up into his face.

He stopped speaking. For a moment she thought she'd given herself away, but when his brows quirked enquiringly she knew with a great rush of relief that he hadn't discerned her tumbling, fevered thoughts.

'And so you think the social organisation of the dolphins here will be similar to those you're accustomed to,' he said.

Ianthe bought time with a bright, meaningless smile. 'It seems a logical assumption. I've just had a great day talking to your museum staff—I had no idea the dolphins were so important in Illyria's folklore. I found the prophecy that as long as the dolphins live Illyria will have a prince interest-ing.'

'Almost every royalist culture has a similar belief,' he said negligently. 'The British have the superstition that the crown will endure as long as the ravens stay at the Tower of London. Fortunately the fishermen on the lake protected the dolphins from those who wanted to persecute them.' He surveyed her distressed face. 'Not everyone sees animal life as sacred.'

A man who had been hovering politely stepped forward. Alex gave him a quick nod and said, 'I'm afraid I must go now. I wish you the best of luck with your work.'

'Thank you,' she said quietly, hoping for—what? One last glance? A significant smile? Some sop for her starving heart to convey that she was somehow special for him?

It didn't happen, of course.

Her mouth curved in a small, bitter smile as she made her way through the crowd to the corner where Bill, his red hair conspicuous, was holding forth. He looked up and gave her a slight, rather smug grin. Although she disliked his assumption that she'd been working her wiles on Alex, her sore heart lifted a little.

It wasn't just the Illyrians who believed in families, she thought. At least when they were working, the team became her family.

Well before midnight Ianthe opened the door into her big, sparsely furnished bedroom in the guesthouse. In spite of the formal name, the reception had been quite informal, without the footmen in satin tights and powdered hair she'd half expected.

Not that Alex needed such accoutrements; his natural authority marked him out.

And now, she told herself as she cleaned her face and scrubbed her teeth, the worst really was over. She only had to get through the next few weeks, and then she could hurry home to New Zealand to nurse her shattered dreams in peace.

Too much raced around her brain—too many thoughts, too many memories—for sleep to come quickly. As night swept over Illyria, as the noise of the city died and the guards in the castle performed some ceremony that involved shouts and drumbeats, she lay wide-eyed and restless, her mind a chaos of fragmentary thoughts driven by demons over and over the same ground.

Royalty—and the very rich and powerful—often didn't live by the same standards as the rest of humankind. They married for practical reasons and found sexual satisfaction in other, illicit relationships.

Alex was both royal and rich and powerful.

He expected to marry well—the presence of the aristocratic Lady Sophie, well chaperoned by his mother, was proof of that.

Did he plan to satisfy his carnal appetites with a practical liaison? Was that what that burning look had meant? He had wanted her in New Zealand; did he think this was a good chance to take up where they had left off?

No, she thought, repelled and sickened by the idea. You're making too much of one glance.

But he wanted her.

And if he did—what the hell was she going to do? Because she hungered for him with a violence that ached through her from the bones out; more than anything in this world she wanted to uncage the consuming desire that prowled behind the fragile bars of her self-control, release it and ride it to consummation and the small, temporary death of physical satiation.

Rolling over onto her side, she wooed her rigid, expectant body to relax by counting and breathing until she could think again.

She loved Alex—had loved him, she thought with a shocked surprise, right from the beginning—and to embark on a clandestine affair with him would corrupt her in some irretrievable way.

Driven eventually from her bed, she paced over to a window. Since she'd met Alex, she thought grimly, she'd spent too many hours looking out of windows, like a woman imprisoned in a tower by her own weakness. It took her a moment to orient herself; she had to sift through her mental direction-finder before she realised that she was staring up into the castle. High above the walls, light burned through three uncurtained windows.

Alex?

No, she thought, angry and scornful with herself. He was probably sleeping soundly, with or without Lady Sophie.

If he asked her to be his mistress, she wondered dismally, what would she say?

Jerkily she twitched the curtains closed again and went back to the bed, determined to sleep.

She'd hoped that this journey to Illyria would close off the past, put a seal on those days when she'd fallen prey to Alex's dark attraction. Instead she'd headed inevitably into the dangerous, destructive battlefield of unrequited love.

Eventually she dozed off, to wake in the clutches of a dream, ridiculous, disconnected as only dreams can be. She'd been swimming with dolphins, intoxicated by her ability to dive and laugh and talk with them, and by her freedom in their watery realm.

Until they looked at her with Alex's eyes and swam away, leaving her calling after them, drowning without them...

'Panda eyes,' Bill teased her over the breakfast table.

'I know, I couldn't sleep. But don't worry, tonight I'll crash.'

'Too much excitement,' he said. 'You and the prince seemed to have a lot to talk about.'

'Dolphins. They're extremely important to the people here.' Her voice was cool and steady, but Bill gave her a swift look.

'Very symbolic,' he said, nodding. 'We won't hurt any sensibilities—it's rather hard to be frivolous or cynical about dolphins. Some of the prince's advisers are suggesting a tourism plan with the dolphins as a centrepiece, but when I asked Alex Considine himself about it he was very non-committal.'

The cameraman leaned over to snaffle a piece of toast and said, 'You'd think he'd be dead keen to drag people in, the more the merrier. Illyria looks pretty poverty-stricken.'

Bill shrugged. 'It is, and he definitely wants to turn it into the ideal little capitalist state, but on his terms. The communist hierarchy used it as a big hunting preserve, so they made no effort to modernise its infrastructure except for their own ends. The prince has got a huge job ahead of him, and he didn't get to the top of the software market by being stupid or hasty. He's going to make damned sure that Illyria ends up the sort of country he intends. He's seen the mistakes other rulers have made, and he's not going to have them happen in his little piece of territory.'

'Then I'm surprised he's letting a film unit in,' Ianthe said with a snap. 'If he's keeping his principality so firmly under his thumb—'

'He's had us checked out, you can guarantee, and he's well aware we're not some Hollywood extravaganza with the possibility of drugs and booze and indiscriminate sleeping around. He knows we're a responsible, intellectually rigorous film crew with a bundle of awards under our belt.' He looked around the table. 'We're leaving in half an hour, so make sure you're ready.'

The half-hour dragged. Staying so close to the castle—wondering where Lady Sophie had spent the night—undermined Ianthe's will. Every time she looked up some part of the castle forced itself into her field of vision. Once she was out of town, she thought hopefully, she'd be all right.

Better, anyway.

A cavalcade of taxis and one large black van waited for them in the forecourt.

'There's the courier,' Bill told Ianthe as they came out through the door. 'He'll be smoothing the way, so to speak. All laid on for us by the prince.'

After she'd been introduced to Lucio, the courier—a thin, gangly man with a squint and a charming smile—he indicated with a flowing gesture of his arm that they should climb into the cars. Most did, waiting more or less patiently as the cameraman and sound recordist went into their usual fuss over their precious pieces of equipment.

To the right the old, curved walls of the castle loomed grimly. Although Ianthe kept her eyes averted it took up so much space that she couldn't ignore it. After a few minutes she realised that she was sitting very still—as still, she thought with a desperate attempt at irony, as a hunted animal—while the alien sun of Illyria burned into her shoulder and arm. Half a world away it had been early autumn; here spring warmed the soft, freshly scented air.

At last the men had packed their equipment to their satisfaction, although the cameraman, she noted with a small smile, had elected to ride with his gear. They climbed into the vehicles and set off through narrow streets—the same streets that a year ago had been packed with people, their faces ecstatic as they'd rushed their prince into the cathedral to crown him.

Coming to Illyria had taught her to hope again, and now she'd have to go through the whole wretched, soul-wrenching process of disengagement once more.

Once she'd left the city—away from Alex and the ever-present castle—surely this aching pain would ease in the busy confusion of filming.

It didn't happen like that.

Oh, she was busy enough. Searching for the dolphins and filming them took time and her whole attention. Although much more timid than the ones she was accustomed to, she managed to forge a relationship with a pod until they became used to the boat and to her, and allowed her into the water with them. Fascinated, Ianthe got drawn more and more into the mystery that was the dolphins' lives, and filming went well, with enough minor setbacks to appease Bill's cruel gods.

But behind her pleasure at working, a nagging darkness ambushed her emotions.

Nobody said anything, although sometimes in those first few weeks, when she noticed Bill watching her with a frown, she'd have to laugh and joke and try to be her usual self.

Illyria in spring was glorious, an eager torrent of life hurtling up the mountains from the valley to banish the grey clouds of winter with a rising wash of colour. The lake sparkled, the gardens around the golden stone houses in the village blossomed, and the sun beamed benignly down on every day.

'Perfect filming weather,' Bill gloated.

Good, Ianthe thought; the sooner we get it finished, the sooner I can get away from here—and away from the regular inspections by Alex that Bill had just warned her had now been scheduled.

The men lived in a lodge in the small fishing village, next door to the apartment Ianthe had been assigned.

'So you can be private,' Lucio had told her, frowning anxiously at the narrow, outside staircase to the first storey rooms.

'It's lovely,' she'd assured him.

She enjoyed the privacy, but more, she enjoyed the people who lived beneath her. Whenever she went up or down the staircase there always seemed to be someone— the woman of the house, or the grandmother, bent-backed and almost toothless, or the two small children—busy in the geranium-filled courtyard.

At first they were shy, but when she greeted them they warmed to her, laughing at her attempts with their language. Robustly enthusiastic, they had no hesitation in correcting her pronunciation, and insisted she spoke only Illyrian to them so that she added enormously to her vocabulary.

The villagers found the whole idea of filming suspicious, and the courier had to explain several times that this was done with their prince's permission, but soon—probably after the fishermen had reported that they made no attempt to kill the dolphins—they began to trust the unit. They gathered in crowds whenever anything was filmed on land, and eventually joined in with gusto when Bill treated them as extras on a film set.

Ianthe was glad that she'd packed her most conventional clothes. Thirty years under a repressive, atheistic regime hadn't stifled their convictions about what was right and what was wrong, and the women still dressed very decorously.

They didn't seem to mind her wetsuit, although she was always careful to shrug into a robe as soon as she emerged from the water. For the rest she wore skirts and shirts and hats, wondering how long it would take for these friendly, noisy, cheerful people to become accustomed to the sight of tourists in scanty bathing suits.

It depended on whether Alex planned to encourage tourism. In a way it would be a pity, she thought, lying sleepless in her bed the night before his first visit to the unit. Illyria's beauty wrung her heart, but even Alex's enormous fortune wasn't enough to modernise it. No doubt he'd choose industries that would make as little impact on the country as possible, but any kind of progress meant change.

She turned onto her stomach. Over dinner Bill had reminded them that Alex would be with them on the following day, and warned them that the prince wanted it to be an informal occasion.

Ianthe wanted to run away—disappear into the blackness of the night and surface in New Zealand and never return. Coward, she thought scornfully, getting out of bed. You're a cowardly wimp—lovesick and pathetic! Grow up.

She looked out of her window, mocking that image she'd had of herself locked in a tower, able only to experience life from behind glass. Most of the buildings were already dark, although she could see several dimly illuminated squares. Fresh, sweet air—filled with the scent of flowers and made crisp by the presence of the large body of water—flowed around her, cooling her heated cheeks.

From there she could see the lake; leaning forward, she watched as something ruffled the smooth surface. No wind breathed across her face or whispered in the trees. It could be the dolphins, she thought, straining to peer through the night.

Even if they weren't there, perhaps a walk would burn off the restlessness in her.

Ten minutes later she was moving quietly past the stone buildings, under the trees in the plaza, past the fishing boats drawn up on the tideless sand.

Inevitably she remembered another lake, smaller than this. Frowning, she strode on. She was suffering from a surfeit of romanticism—she hadn't had a chance to really get to know Alex, after all. His personality was so overwhelming she'd just surrendered to it, and fallen into the trap of glamorising the few days they'd had together.

Except, she thought wistfully, that it wasn't Alex the Rich and Powerful, Alex the Prince, she'd fallen in love with. It was the man, and she knew what he was like. Authoritative, a little arrogant, brave, strong...

And compassionate, and honourable. He hadn't made love to her then because he'd known there'd be no place for her in his life. Had he decided that perhaps there was a place, after all? A discreet place, of course, well out of the public eye...

Her heart twisted. No, she thought strongly. I love him, but I'm worth more than that.

A swirl of water—a sharp *clop* as something broke the surface—jerked her back to her surroundings. She stopped and peered out across the water, noting the telltale disturbance that indicated dolphins.

From the corner of her eye she caught a flicker of movement along the beach. Suddenly a little afraid, she swivelled around and, although he was a hundred metres away in the darkness, she knew immediately who walked towards her. Unable to hear the soft lap of the waves for the heady drumbeat of her pulses, she waited, remembering another night and another lake a world away, and the man who had waited for her cloaked then, as he was now, in starshine and darkness.

'Alex,' she whispered as he came up to her.

He smiled, his teeth a white flash in the night. 'I think I could die listening to you saying my name like that.'

She asked, 'Where is Lady Sophie?'

'In England,' he said evenly. 'You've walked a long way from the village. Does your leg hurt?'

Surprised to see how far away the little cluster of lights was, she swallowed to steady her voice. 'No, it's fine; I made sure I got into shape before I went back to the Bay of Islands, and I've kept exercising.'

'Good,' he said, but distantly, as though he had other things on his mind.

Of course he did, she thought. There you go again, attaching far too much importance to everything he says.

He broke into her recriminations by saying, 'Sophie is the daughter of a friend, nothing more. She came for a short holiday because she has a broken heart. And, no, I didn't break it. She's decided to go back and face up to things instead of running away.'

Rapidly, jealously, she demanded, 'And what about the Frenchwoman?'

'Gossip,' he said impatiently. 'Ianthe, you know perfectly well that people gossip. It's one of the things you dislike so much about fame.'

'Is it worse now that you're a reigning prince?'

'In Illyria most of it is kindly. I don't care about the rest of the world.'

No, of course not. Only Alex, she thought almost incoherently, had enough confidence to be able to ignore the tissue of supposition and inference and outright lies that were spun around the newsworthy. He was master of his world.

He said, 'What do you think of Illyria, now that you've been here a whole month?'

She could answer that sincerely. 'I love it. It's beautiful, and the people are so friendly—they've almost completely accepted us now.'

'I hoped you'd like it,' he said, his voice deepening. 'Ianthe, look at me.'

With dilated eyes she looked up. Pale starlight picked out the dark gloss of hair and the disciplined strength of his features.

She swallowed an enormous lump in her throat.

'I know it's too early,' he said, his voice sensual and rough, a note of self-derision colouring each word as he went on, 'I planned to wait for at least another couple of weeks—if we hadn't met like this I probably could have done it.'

Here it was. He was going to ask her to be his mistress. Ianthe pressed her hand against her heart, as though to keep it in place.

He finished, 'But you manage to smash through every flimsy defence I put up. I can't wait any longer.'

'Alex—don't.' The words grated, emerged hard and cold and stony.

There was silence, and then he asked harshly, 'Am I wrong?'

'Please,' she whispered.

He silenced her with a touch on her arm, and turned her towards him. The soft stars lent enough light for him to see the tears in her eyes.

'Ianthe,' he said, rasping out the word. 'For God's sake, Ianthe, my little love, don't cry. I knew it was a gamble to get you here—knowing how you'd hate the life—but I hoped…'

Ianthe looked at him, chilled by the icy composure in his eyes, and then—as though someone had ripped down a curtain—recognised the immense self-control it took for him to maintain it. Her heart overflowed and she caught back an enormous sob.

'It's all right,' he said roughly. The hawkish features hardened into an implacable mask.

Desperate to get rid of that bleakness, Ianthe said, 'I love you so much that I'll live with you for ever, but won't your people despise you if you have a mistress?'

He said fiercely, 'I don't want you to be my mistress! God, when I think how I've struggled and bled not to contact you, because it wouldn't be fair—knowing how you felt about the sort of life I have to live...' He stopped, then demanded incredulously, 'You'd be my mistress?'

'Yes.' It came out half-strangled but definite.

And suddenly that self-control was shattered, and his eyes were no longer the colour of ice under the moon. In a low, unyielding voice he said, 'I love you. I've loved you since I first set eyes on you, I think. Certainly within half an hour. I looked at you and the world splintered into shards, like a glass bauble hit by a stone. Somehow, without even trying, you found a place for yourself in my heart's core, and although I've tried for your sake to evict you, I haven't been able to do it. Ianthe, the last day we had together in New Zealand you said that we didn't really know each other—'

'I was trying to convince myself,' she said, still unable to believe that he meant what he had just said.

'Do you still believe it?'

'No. I've been waiting for you all my life.'

'And I for you.' He stood very straight, almost as though bracing himself. The dark, arrogant head was held high, but his voice was uneven as he said, 'Ianthe, will you do me the honour of being my wife? I know you'll find life difficult here—'

Passionately, at last beginning to believe what she'd heard, she said, 'Oh, Alex, of course I'll marry you! I love Illyria, but even if I didn't—I'll be with you, and that's all I want now.'

He flung back his head and laughed, the triumphant sound echoing across the water. Then he kissed her, his mouth demanding, seeking, his arms iron bars around her.

CHAPTER TEN

IANTHE thought the world stood still. She thought the stars swung wildly and the mountains swooped, and somehow through the fires of delight she heard a loud swish from the lake.

Alex lifted his head; together they turned. There, leaping in formation, were the pod of dolphins she'd been cultivating. They swam past, turned, and swam back again before disappearing into the night.

Shaken, almost shocked, Ianthe said, 'I—I thought I saw them before, from my window. That's why I came down.'

'I saw them too. Do you think they fancy themselves as matchmakers?' He spoke tenderly, with something of the awe she felt. 'I think they gave us their approval, don't you?'

'I think they did.' Oddly shy, she looked up, saw him smile openly, without reservation. 'What happens now?'

He said levelly, 'I take you back to the village. Are you on schedule for filming?'

She nodded, repressing the disappointment that coursed through her. 'We weren't expecting you until tomorrow. Are you staying here?'

He smiled and took her hands, holding them lightly in his. Acutely, expectantly alive, thrilling with a mixture of emotions so powerful she couldn't separate them—a heady combination of enormous joy and relief and the desire that prowled restlessly through her—she waited for him to speak.

'I have a villa around the next headland,' he said. 'I couldn't sleep, and I thought—foolishly, because of course it wouldn't happen—that somehow you were calling me.

170

So I came and sat on a rock, thinking, *She is along there. One of those lights might be hers. Tomorrow I'll be seeing her.* And there, like Aphrodite, you were, coming towards me across the sand.' He gave an ironic little laugh. 'I expected roses to bloom under your feet—or violets, like your name.'

She said, 'I felt like death.'

'You must have known I loved you,' he said urgently.

'No. I knew you *wanted* me.'

'So you thought I'd brought you here to be my mistress.' His voice was level, yet beneath it lurked a note of grimness.

'Brought me here?'

'Didn't you realise?' he said with amused mockery. 'Why else would I have told a trusted aide to contact Fenn's production company and suggest he do something about the dolphins?'

'I didn't know,' she said. 'Bill didn't tell me!'

'He didn't know himself, although he might have suspected after you got here. I was very discreet, but I had to see you again and that seemed the best way.'

'Did you tell him I had to front the documentary?' she asked, trying to tug her hand away.

His fingers tightened around hers. 'I didn't appear in the negotiations at all,' he said, a note of exasperation roughening his voice.

'That's an evasion.' She had been so happy the moment before—she was still happy—but the knowledge that she hadn't come to Illyria because of her own abilities ate like a worm into the heart of her happiness. 'You didn't have to go to such extremes—if you'd just asked me I'd have come. I don't appear to have any pride where you're concerned.'

'Stop it,' he commanded sternly. He took her stiff, resistant body in his arms and said with leashed, uncompromising determination, 'You're too proud. Listen to me; Bill suggested you. He said—and my very discreet aide told me

these were his exact words—that you were the only person
he'd consider using because you're a real pro, and because
you have this astonishing empathy with dolphins. Why are
you so insecure about your abilities?'

'I'm not. I'm a good scientist—'

'That's not all you are.' Giving her a little shake, he said
judicially, 'You're heart-shakingly beautiful, you're kind
and sensible and extremely intelligent, your smile can be
shy or gleeful or intently, passionately vivid, your laugh
twists my heart and your voice does unmentionable things
to my libido—why can't you accept that? Your father really
did a number on you, didn't he?'

Startled by his perception, she muttered, 'All right, so
when he left I was shattered. But I've grown up now.'

His arms tightened around her. The insistent pressure of
his need summoned a swift response, heat flooding through
her.

'I think,' he said, 'there's a small girl deep inside you
who still believes that it's her fault her father left.'

His perceptiveness made her uneasy. Was he always going to read her so clearly? In a way it made her feel naked,
exposed. Then she looked up and saw love in his eyes, and
that frightened part of her was soothed. She could trust him,
she thought dizzily. 'Just as there's a small boy inside you
who believes that duty and responsibility are the most important things in his life?'

His mouth curled into a swift white smile. *'Touché.'*

'If I'd decided not to come, what would you have done
then?'

'I thought of kidnapping you,' he said prosaically, his
hand tightening on her back.

She gave a choked laugh. 'All you had to do was ask!'

'Ah, but I didn't know that.'

Anger gone, she kissed his throat, inhaling that subtle
scent, the essence of his masculinity. 'How could you not?
You must know how I feel about you—you knew before

you left New Zealand.' A soft breath of wind teased a strand of hair across Ianthe's face.

He brushed the tress back behind her ear. Quietly, the steadiness of his voice almost intimidating, he said, 'I knew you wanted me. At first I thought that was all it was. And I tried very hard to believe that all I felt was an overwhelming desire. But I hadn't been away from you more than a few days when I realised how wrong I'd been.'

Nodding, she sighed. 'I know. Me too.'

He pulled her close, so close that she gasped before giving him the warm promise of her mouth, the unspoken surrender that he wanted.

Too soon he broke the kiss to rest his chin on the top of her head. Unsteadily he said, 'About a week after I'd arrived in Illyria I decided that I'd give myself a year to tidy things up here, and then I'd ask you over. I wanted you to see Illyria, understand what it would be like to live here, before you made your choice. And, so that it wouldn't embarrass you, I thought the best way would be to use the dolphins.'

'Machiavelli,' she teased.

'Oh, I can wheel and deal with the best of them. It's been the longest, hardest year of my life, because although I knew I loved you I didn't know how it was for you.' He laughed quietly. 'I must admit, I was cheered by your behaviour when you got here. You were very stiff, very formal, and your beautiful golden eyes glittered with sparks whenever I happened to look at poor Sophie!'

'I was in deepest despair,' she said mournfully.

'I would hate to see you when you're angry.' His voice was amused, almost ironic. 'So—do you think you can be happy here in Illyria?'

She said with complete conviction, 'I can be happy anywhere with you.'

'Well, unless the Illyrians decide that they want some other form of government, it will be this country for the rest of our lives. You've started well; I hear that you're already able to make yourself understood in the language.'

'Barely!'

'That's not what I'm told. You have a charming accent, and you're getting on very well with the villagers.'

'You've got a spy—Lucio!' she said, smiling into his shoulder.

He said curtly, 'Not a spy. You needed someone to liaise with the villagers, and I wanted to make sure that the filming went well, but most of all I needed to know that you were happy.'

A long finger tipped her chin and he looked at her with such open, hungry need that she shivered.

'I hoped that you'd learn to like the people,' he said.

And that they'd like me? But she didn't voice the thought as she lowered her head to kiss his fingers.

Deeply, his voice uneven, he said, 'I knew they'd like you. But Lucio says you seem to enjoy their company.'

'I do—very much.'

He kissed her again with such famished intensity that she was sure the barriers had at last been lowered. But even though she followed him into the honeyed, perfumed land of the senses that was their realm alone, she sensed that he was still holding back. And she thought she knew why.

This time when he lifted his head and reluctantly let her go, she said, 'Alex, I said a lot about hating to live so publicly, but I didn't realise—I didn't know that that was going to be your life.' She glanced up at his angular profile. 'Loving you makes a terrific difference. I'll probably get used to living publicly, but I'd never get used to being without you.'

A muscle flicked in his jaw. He took her hand and began to walk her across the sand—back, she noticed with a shiver of frustration, towards the village. After a moment he said, 'This last year has shown me just how cold and dreary life is without you. However, there's something else

I should confess to. When I left New Zealand I had to make sure that you were safe and happy.'

She suddenly understood what he meant. 'So you provided the sponsorship money?'

'Yes,' he said. His voice hardened. 'I had to, my heart. I wanted you to be happy—not too happy without me, but I was almost certain that you'd got over the worst of your phobia and I knew you'd want to get back to your dolphins. So I organised the money for you.'

She should have been furious. 'I have a horrid suspicion that you could do anything in the world and I'd forgive you. But you do realise that I'll expect you to sponsor the person who takes my place there? Actually, I have a good idea who it'll be. The graduate student who's taking my place at the moment is already in love with the pod, and the dolphins like her a lot too.'

Their footsteps slowed, stopped. He said thickly, 'Of course I will—you can do whatever you want! Everything I am, everything I have, is worth nothing to me if I can't make you happy.'

'Then why,' she asked, 'are we going back to the village?'

His hand tightened on hers. Flatly he said, 'Darling, although I want to take you back to my villa and make love to you until the stars fall from the sky, we can't. We'll announce our engagement when you finish here, and get married in a couple of months' time. Unfortunately that's how long it will take to organise. Until then you'll have to stay with my mother—she wants to take you under her wing, and there are things you'll have to learn: protocol, who's who, court behaviour. We'll have no time alone.' He kissed the palm of her hand, then bit the small mound under her thumb.

'Oh,' she said, flushing. 'I thought—'

He laughed softly, without humour. 'Illyrians are old-fashioned, and your reputation is important. That's why I left the castle that first night, and why from now on we'll only ever be together when there are other people around.'

She stared at him. 'Alex,' she said in a small voice, 'I'm not a virgin.'

His eyes held hers. 'Neither am I.'

She said, 'Greg was another marine biologist and I was engaged to him. When he went to Papua New Guinea to study the Sepik River estuary, he got some tropical bug. They couldn't even get him to a hospital, but the doctor said it wouldn't have made any difference if they had. He was dead within twenty-four hours.'

He said, 'It must have been hell for you.'

Her mouth twisted. 'It was hell for him.'

'I'd be lying if I said I didn't mind. I've never been possessive with women before, but I'm possessive with you.' He reined something hot and undeniable back, looking at her with eyes that smouldered. 'Your life previously has made you what you are. You haven't asked me about the fact that I'm definitely not a virgin; I don't see any need to explore your past.' His lean hands stroked across her shoulders. 'The future is what interests me now,' he said, and kissed her with fierce, hard concentration.

Ianthe wanted passion, she wanted to lie beneath him in some huge bed and journey with him into the dangerous pleasure of the senses. His mouth ravaged hers and she yielded, but almost immediately the famished desperation was leashed and he lifted his head, saying unevenly, 'Not yet, my darling, my love. Not yet. But we'll have our time together, I promise.'

Bells all over the little city clanged joyously, many out of tune, all proclaiming the Illyrians' delight in the wedding and coronation, for after pronouncing them man and wife the bishop crowned Ianthe with a silver crown of a design so antique that she looked like something from a fabled icon. Baroque pearls formed dolphins and mermaids around it, with sapphires glinting between.

Then the bells went mad, and through the open doors of the cathedral she heard a wild cheering, and for a moment her eyes dilated.

Alex took her hand and squeezed it. Gratefully she returned the pressure, her terror dissipating like rain on a summer's day.

Together they walked down the aisle and out onto the steps. As they appeared in the sunlight the roar of cheering swelled to a crescendo. While they'd been in the cathedral a carpet of fir branches had been laid to form a pathway to the open carriage. Their fresh green scent rose to meet them, reminding Ianthe of the pines around the lake in New Zealand.

'To keep our marriage evergreen,' Alex said when they were seated in the carriage.

She hugged the thought all the way up to the castle, and during the formal breakfast. After that there was a ritual breaking of bread with people from the poorest quarters— mostly children, who fell silent in awe as she approached them.

Important for symbolism, Ianthe agreed as she crouched by a small child in a wheelchair and coaxed a shy smile, but even more important was the legal trust Alex had established in their names—a trust to dispense money to sponsor children at school and university.

And then it was over. At last she and Alex would be alone. Trying out her still primitive Illyrian, she said, 'Should I go now?' to Alex's mother.

'Yes, it is time,' she said, and smiled at Ianthe's stepmother, who'd asked a little diffidently if she could come up and help her dress. Surprised, but pleased, Ianthe had agreed, and now all three women made their way to the door.

A maid waited. Alex's mother said, 'Great joy, Ianthe,' and went back to her guests.

They had come to know each other well these past two months, and to respect each other. Serena Considine hid

her innate toughness under an elegant, aristocratic demean-
our, and although she must have wondered at her son's
determination to marry a nobody, she had never let Ianthe
see any foreboding or worry.

In the room she'd soon share with Alex, her stepmother
and the maid got her out of the slender, graceful wedding
dress designed by an Illyrian couturier who had moved to
Paris. Made of cream silk tulle, it hadn't overpowered her
slender body, and its simplicity had set off the antique lace
veil she wore.

To go away she'd chosen a suit coloured the pure copper
of the highlights in her hair, and she was examining her
reflection with a critical, anxious eye when someone
knocked on the door.

'You look wonderful,' her stepmother said, and gave her
a kiss on the cheek. 'Be happy, Ianthe, as happy as I've
been with your father.'

The maid opened the door. 'Ready?' Alex asked.

Smiling, Ianthe went to meet him. 'Very ready.'

His gaze rested a taut second on her mouth. 'The worst
is over,' he said. 'Only a few more minutes now.'

Together they went down the stairs. Guests poured
through the doors into the hall of the castle; there was a
flurry of good wishes, much throwing of rose petals and
sugared almonds, and then they were in a car being driven
along streets that were still lined with waving, yelling
Illyrians, their flushed faces delighted, their upraised arms
making the only kind of guard of honour Ianthe valued.

'We'll change cars at a hunting lodge not far from here,'
Alex told her on the outskirts of the city. 'I'll drive from
then on.' They were honeymooning in Illyria, but Alex had
refused to tell her where, beyond saying that it would be a
very casual holiday.

The road wound around the lake for some kilometres
before climbing the side of a low mountain and diving into
a small valley. On one side was a thick forest, and it was

into this that the road turned, leaving the brilliant sunlight to plunge into sweet-smelling dimness.

The hunting lodge, far from being the turreted and walled Middle European fantasy that Ianthe had imagined, turned out to be a splendid Palladian villa set on a low eminence so that the sun picked out its glorious proportions and the mellow stone with a tender, unerring eye. At the foot of a tier of shallow steps stood a Range Rover.

No one emerged from the columned entrance when the car stopped in front of it. The chauffeur leapt out and smiled encouragingly at Ianthe as he opened her door. Heart beating high and rapidly in her breast, Ianthe waited, admiring the steps leading up to the wide wooden doors—or were they bronze?—while their luggage was transferred into the other vehicle.

And then at last they were alone.

'Where are we going?' Ianthe asked as they drew away from the lodge.

'Somewhere very private.' Until then Alex hadn't touched her, but at this he picked up her hand and kissed the inside of her wrist. 'Close to the place where I spent the first ten years of my life,' he said calmly.

'I thought that was by the lake.'

'Not this one,' he said. 'My lake is much smaller.'

'I still find it difficult to believe that you lived here for ten years without being betrayed.'

'When the communists took over, my mother and father were newly-weds, holidaying where we're going. They couldn't get out—not even over the mountains—because there was a guerilla war going on. I doubt if it would have been an option, anyway, because my father felt very strongly that he had no right to leave his people. So he stayed, and my mother wouldn't leave him, and eventually I was born.'

No wonder the Illyrians loved Alex's mother. 'And then somebody talked?'

He nodded. 'Somebody talked. At least we were warned

that they were coming to take us away to be re-educated. My father knew there was no hope of us escaping without a diversion. He didn't expect the locals to do it—they had relatives who'd been taken hostage. So he created a diversion himself, and gave my mother and me time to climb into Italy.'

'And you never knew what happened to him.'

'I do now. He was caught and killed,' he said evenly. 'Along with about fifty of the villagers.'

Ianthe made a distressed noise.

'It's a long time ago, but it's one of the main reasons I decided to come back—even though I believed I was giving up any chance of marrying you,' he said soberly. 'I couldn't abandon them again—they had kept the faith with us. And I owed it, I felt, to my father's memory.'

He wouldn't be the man she loved if he'd taken the easy option. 'I do understand,' she said.

As they drove through the smiling fields and woodlands, they talked of the changes Alex intended to make—improving the transport system being a major aim—and whether he could bring his small state into the modern world without losing all that made it so special.

At last they followed a pass between the shoulders of two mountains and from the top saw another lake, small and exquisitely beautiful. The road turned into a narrow track that dived down between thick forests to the lakeside.

The house was long and low and modern, built of local materials so that it fitted comfortably into the scenery, but it wasn't until she walked across the tiled floor and out onto the terrace that Ianthe realised what he'd done.

'Oh—Alex!' she breathed.

In front of her, facing south and overlooking the glowing, shimmering waters of the lake, was a wide bench with white canvas cushions and wicker lounges beneath a vine-covered pergola.

He said from behind her, 'I wanted you to have somewhere that reminds you of New Zealand. We'll be able to get here quite often, and it will be a good place for children.'

'Oh, Alex,' she said again, fighting back the sudden sting of tears.

'You've given up so much,' he said.

She shook her head. 'I've given up *nothing*,' she said passionately. 'Nothing that I haven't gained back many more times over. All I want is you.'

Although his hands on her shoulders were gentle, she sensed the great strength kept under rigorous restraint.

She kissed one of his hands and then the other, before turning around. Something—neither fear nor exactly anticipation—kicked in her stomach as she met his gleaming eyes. Laughing deep in his throat, he kissed the spot where her neck joined her shoulder, lingering over the juncture until heat poured through her.

Ianthe lifted her face, tasting the place in his jaw where a muscle flicked, once, twice, three times. His scent, potent yet faint, teased her nerves, honing the swift tide of desire into an urgent torrent.

He stood very still, and then he drew a sharp breath and kissed her with a starving ferocity that sent her head reeling. It was what she wanted, though. Oh, yes, this was what she'd been waiting for—this need for completion had ached inside her for too long.

Lifting her, he carried her back inside, into a room where he put her down on the bed. Unsteadily he said, 'I want to make it tender for you, take you slowly, but I can't—I need you so much—'

But he did. He made love to her with a drowning absorption, as though he'd never before endured such rapture, and she responded with the same intensity, caught up in the dark whirlwind of their passion. At length, when he had taken her clothes from her and caressed her into frenzy, he moved over her.

Ianthe's eyes had been closed with languorous delight. Now she opened them, and saw through her heavy lashes the face of hunger, the stripped, elemental angles that denoted his desperate need.

Something wild and primitive burst into flame inside her; she flung her arms back and let him look his fill, and then, when the skin along his high cheekbones flushed darkly, she said, 'Now. Now. Right now.'

He was exquisitely careful until, tormented to madness, she twisted beneath him and pulled him down, enclosing him, taking him into her. It was like riding a storm, like flinging herself into the heart of a cyclone, like soaring into a crystalline midnight sky on winds of flame.

Ravished by sensation, by the stark, explosive nature of her response, Ianthe found herself straining for something else, for something more, and more and more, until suddenly she was tossed into an implosion of delight, a soaring, magnificent rapture that loosened the bonds of the world.

And Alex went with her, his arms locking her to him as they found the heart of the sun.

Much later—when they had slept, and the sky outside was garnished with the soft splendour of stars—he said lazily, 'I hope to be the last prince of Illyria. If all goes well the people will take control over their own destinies before I die, and our children will be able to do what they want to.'

Ianthe wondered about that. It didn't seem likely that the Illyrians' devotion to their ruling family would be wiped out in one generation. Reaching up, she bit gently into the hard swell of his shoulder muscle, and then delicately, daintily, licked the salty skin.

'I'm not worrying about that,' she said, answering his unspoken words. 'Suddenly I don't care much about the future. The present is far too exciting.'

He lay very still, and beneath her cheek she could feel his heart pick up speed. However, he said uncompromisingly, 'Stop trying to seduce me. I need to say this. I know that marrying me is a massive deviation from *your* career path, but at least you can study the dolphins here.'

'Alex,' she said quietly, walking her fingers lightly down the taut muscles of his stomach, 'I chose you. The dolphins are a very nice bonus, but if there hadn't been any here I'd have stayed just the same. I could have turned my back on you and on Illyria, and stayed with my dolphins in the Bay of Islands, but love means that you choose a person, and usually when you make a choice you have to give other things up. You did that when you decided to come back to Illyria. Deciding to stay with you was easy once I'd realised that I didn't much enjoy the life I was leading without you. I love you—it's as straightforward as that. Your father loved you and your mother enough to sacrifice his life for you—I feel the same way.'

His chest lifted in a great breath. Startled, she looked up. To her astonishment his eyes were wet, the lashes thick and spiky against the mesmerising blue, his face bare of everything but the pressure of unbearable emotion.

His arms crushed her to him. He said nothing for a long time, and when at last he spoke his voice was low and shaken. 'My life is nothing—*nothing*—without you. I've always believed in love—my mother and father were lovers, and he literally sacrificed his life for ours. I would die for you, but I never—for some reason I never expected to be loved as my mother loved my father.'

She struggled a moment and he loosened his grip. Holding his face in her hands, she said evenly, 'I love you more than I've loved anything else in my life. I didn't really believe in love. Oh, I knew it existed—my father and my stepmother are very happy together, and I used to envy Tricia because her parents laughed together and were so kind to each other. But I grew up thinking that love came with too big a price tag—until I met you. And when you went away I realised that I was ready to pay the price.'

'I knew it was something,' he said, turning his head to kiss her palm. Against the sensitive skin he said, 'You were

so damned elusive. You roused the hunter in me right from
the first but I knew I couldn't follow through. As well as
being beautiful beyond words you were fragile. And I had
to decide whether or not I was coming back to Illyria. I'd
been approached by people who were convinced that the
country could only become healed with me as its ruler, but
I didn't want to give up everything I'd worked so hard to
achieve. And you got in my way, infiltrated my thoughts,
drove me mad with your golden eyes and your white skin
and that honey-coloured hair.'

'I didn't know,' she said slowly, shocked by the raw
emotion in his voice. 'You were so confident and controlled.'

'I tried. I've never had such consuming frustration eating
at my guts, shadowing my dreams—driving me crazy until
I couldn't think, couldn't eat without seeing your face and
hearing your voice. I tried to keep away—I even sent Mark
to check up on you when the cyclone was coming—but it
was no use. I had to see for myself. And you were so
bloody cool!'

'We were both hiding,' she said. 'I knew my feelings
weren't one-sided, but you told me you weren't going to
do anything about it. And I was relieved because I didn't
want to love anyone.'

'Not even the man you were engaged to?'

'I loved Greg, but it was a meagre, rationed sort of
love—I was too afraid of being hurt so I held myself back.
He was a happy man—always laughing, always full of fun.
I don't think he knew just how little he had of me.'

'Poor devil,' he said sombrely.

Ianthe nodded. 'I shiver now when I think of it,' she said
with a bleak intensity, 'because I would have married him
and short-changed us both.'

'If you'd married him I would have found you and taken
you away from him,' Alex said.

Ianthe's eyes met a hot, predatory gaze. Such behaviour
might have been accepted in the Middle Ages, but not now,

not ever. Yet her comment died on her lips. He would, she thought, have done just that.

In some ways Alex was not very civilised.

She said, 'That is profoundly politically incorrect and you know it, but I have a horrible feeling I'd have followed you to the end of the world. That's why I was so wary when I met you, because intuition warned me that you had the power to make me love nakedly, without reservations. You smashed through the protective mechanisms I'd always used, until I had no refuge from my own heart. I suppose that's why I let Bill talk me into coming to Illyria. Oh, I told myself I wanted some sort of closure, but I simply needed to be near you.'

His smile was rakish, more carefree than she'd ever seen it. 'And I went to a lot of trouble to lure you here. I planned to move in on you slowly, cunningly—hunt you down with golden arrows and silken nets and tempting little morsels.'

'Instead you were rude and abrupt, and you even left the castle so that—'

'So that I didn't break down the door and make wild, passionate love to you,' he said lazily, and laughed as heat coloured her skin. 'As for the rudeness—I wasn't expecting you that night. Until then I'd thought that I could keep control, but one look at your tired face and I wanted to kiss all that fatigue away and take you to bed and keep you awake all night.'

'I thought you hated me.'

'I'd promised myself that I wouldn't say anything to you until you'd seen how we live, what sort of people we are—until you had some idea of whether you could bear to spend the rest of your life here.' He spoke deeply, strongly.

'You're too honourable,' she grumbled.

'Hardly. My noble intentions lasted barely a month! When we met on the lake shore every thought of honour and waiting flew straight out of the window. Besides, you hadn't cut your hair—I thought it was a signal, a tiny ray of hope.'

'It was,' she whispered, and kissed his long lashes, and then the beautiful, chiselled edges of his mouth, and found his earlobe, nipping it with care and intense pleasure.

His arm tightened around her. 'If you keep doing that,' he said silkily, 'I might retaliate. I thought, you know, that I wouldn't have children, and then the Illyrians would be forced to find another way. But I want your children.'

By then Ianthe was in no doubt that she took first place in his heart. She ducked her head and kissed the flat male nipple. 'If I keep doing what?' she asked innocently. 'As for our children—they'll find their own paths. Like us.'

From now on her life and Alex's would be braided together so intricately that there would be no unwinding. Not like a braid, she thought—no, more like woven cloth. They'd make their life into a tapestry, grand and glorious and beautiful, woven with love and laughter and hard work and, yes, with the shining threads of desire and passion.

Smiling, she kissed him again.

'That's it,' he said, his eyes glinting with dangerous pleasure. 'I have to retaliate now.'

He told her exactly how he planned to do that, and then he showed her, and she sighed and gave in to the passion he would always rouse. With her last shred of self-possession she thought that as long as they were together they'd have everything they'd ever want.

Romance is just one click away!

online book **serials**

➤ *Exclusive* to our web site, get caught up in both the daily and weekly online installments of new romance stories.

➤ Try the Writing Round Robin. Contribute a chapter to a story created by our members. Plus, winners will get prizes.

romantic **travel**

➤ Want to know where the best place to kiss in New York City is, or which restaurant in Los Angeles is the most romantic? Check out our Romantic Hot Spots for the scoop.

➤ Share your travel tips and stories with us on the romantic travel message boards.

romantic reading **library**

➤ Relax as you read our collection of Romantic Poetry.

➤ Take a peek at the Top 10 Most Romantic Lines!

Visit us online at

www.eHarlequin.com
on Women.com Networks